Barrabas gripped his rifle, eyes scanning the hard faces

He looked at the enemy army. If he was going down, he'd go down firing. Behind him, of a single mind, his soldiers felt the same.

Facing him was the enemy leader, standing with feet apart. The light from the dying flare flickered madly across her face, dissolving against the sweat-soaked fatigues that clung wetly to the curves of her body.

Her face was framed by jet-black hair that fell carelessly over her shoulders. Her shirt, stretched back by the weight of the cartridge belt she wore, revealed a forceful cleavage.

She was the kind of woman men would die for.

Starting now.

Now available in the exciting new series
from Gold Eagle Books

SOBs
by Jack Hild

#1 The Barrabas Run
#2 The Plains of Fire
#3 Butchers of Eden
#4 Show No Mercy

SOBs

SHOW NO MERCY

JACK HILD

A GOLD EAGLE BOOK FROM

WORLDWIDE

TORONTO • NEW YORK • LONDON • PARIS
AMSTERDAM • STOCKHOLM • HAMBURG
ATHENS • MILAN • TOKYO • SYDNEY

First edition January 1985

ISBN 0-373-61604-X

Special thanks and acknowledgment to
Robin Hardy for his contribution to this work

Printed in Canada

1

Twenty-four-hour highway restaurants are the same all over. After the bars close in the villages of the German Saarland, Friday-night action moves to the roadside oases. Bored teenagers hang out with soldiers from the nearby American military base and with any hitchhikers who get trapped in the dead-end nowhere near the French border when daylight fades.

The tall blond man in cowboy boots was let off on the highway near midnight. He had a knapsack and a sign marked Paris. He stuck out his thumb for about an hour. Ten cars passed and none stopped. He went into the all-night restaurant and drank coffee.

Day woke up at 5:00 A.M. A chilly gray fog writhed along the dark green fields rolling through the valleys of southeast Germany.

The blond man stood outside the glass front doors and waited.

Eventually he saw what he was waiting for.

A man and woman left the restaurant and walked to a Land Rover in the parking lot. The man was drunk and leaned heavily on his girlfriend's shoulder for support. He was drawling in loud American English. The woman insisted she would drive.

The blond man waited until they were six feet away. Then he called to them.

"Hey, man, can you help out a fellow American? I've been trying to get to Paris, and I've been stuck here all night."

The drunk man swung around, pivoting off his girl-friend.

"You like the blues?" he asked in a long Southern drawl.

"I love the blues," the blond man called back.

"Then you got yourself a ride." The drunk man swayed against his girlfriend. He looked at her. "That all right with you, honey?"

"Sure." She smiled at the hitchhiker. "Come on. Get in."

In the car the drunk American plunged a cassette into the tape deck. The deep, rich music of the blues flooded the car. The blond man thrust his hand into the front seat.

"Glen Beam," he said. "Much appreciate the ride. It's been a long night."

The drunk man passed a bottle back to him.

"Have some bourbon. Pleased to meet you. Name's Doug. This here's Susan. Susy. Susy Q." He leaned over and rubbed his nose in her neck.

"Stop it! I'm trying to drive." She gave him an affectionate shove. Then to the hitchhiker she said, "We're going to Metz for breakfast. That'll get you over the border into France."

"Yeah," Doug said loudly. "The Friday-night routine. Drink too much. Hang out back there in the restaurant to sober up. Metz for breakfast and back to the base. Nothing else to do in this corner of Germany."

"You guys live in Metz?" Beam was shouting over the music. He passed the bourbon back to Doug.

"Uh-uh." Doug shook his head emphatically. "We're soldiers. We live at the U.S. Army base right up the road here, outside Kaiserslauten. Hey, Susy Q, let's make a quick stop to pick up some Cokes, baby. We need mix for the bourbon."

"You've had enough to drink already." But she put on the blinker and pulled into the exit lane.

Beam sat back, mildly exhilarated by the few swigs of whiskey. It was going to be easier than he had anticipated.

A few minutes later the car was climbing a winding road up the side of one of the forested hills that lined the river valley.

"You got a passport?" Doug asked Beam. "Just show it at the gate. You need some ID."

Beam pulled the document from his knapsack as the car slowed at the high wire fence. There was one guard standing outside the guardhouse.

Doug and Susan flashed their military ID. Beam held his passport aloft. The guard gave it a second look, unsure about it.

Doug tapped at the window and pointed to his ID again. U.S. Army Captain Doug Chalmers had top security clearance. The open sesame of military passes. The guard nodded and waved them through.

The car wound along the slopes of a hill. Through forests on either side of the road, they passed long rows of military equipment parked in fields. Artillery in one field, then jeeps. Another one was full of ambulances. Then a field of tanks. And a field of trucks. Beam was fascinated. There was enough olive-green machinery here to fight a war. He laughed to himself. That was why it was here. To fight wars. NATO versus the Russkies. Millions of dollars' worth of equipment waiting to go into action. Or onto the black market. He sighed. Another time, maybe.

The car pulled onto a level stretch at the top of the hill. Ahead of them, surrounded by more forests, stretched long rows of ugly prefab military barracks.

"Home sweet home," Doug drawled, still slurring his words. "How d'you like it?"

"Well, the setting's nice," said Beam, looking at the forest of pine trees that crowned the hill.

Doug laughed. "Hear that, Susy? He likes the setting." Doug looked back, smiling. "Smartass," he joked.

"I'll get the Cokes," said Susan. She parked alongside one of the barracks and left the car.

Doug leaned back, relaxed, drunk and tired. "Six more months," he said, staring ahead out the windshield. "Then it's back to stateside duty." In the back seat the hitchhiker was quiet. Something made Doug want to look behind him. He started to turn around.

Beam pulled the trigger.

The silenced gun made little noise but a big mess.

Captain Doug Chalmers's head bucked against the side window, then slapped back against the headrest. A long gush of blood blew into the back seat. Beam flicked his hand out of the way. The blood steamed on the cold seat and ran down to the floor, where it formed a puddle on the carpet. In the front seat the dead man's eyes stared glassily out the window.

Beam sat back and waited.

Susan opened the driver's-side door, clutching Cokes in one hand, and climbed in.

"There were only two..." she began.

Beam circled his arm around her mouth and shoved the barrel of the French-made M-50 pistol into her neck. A 9mm parabellum slammed into her brain. It was a better shot. No mess.

The Cokes clattered onto the ground outside the door.

Beam got out, pushed the dead woman's legs into the car and shut the door. The camp was deserted. He picked up a can of Coke, snapped off the tab and took a long swallow.

He walked. He knew exactly where to go.

The truck was almost indistinguishable in the field of trucks, but it was parked at a different angle, away from and off to the side of the others. And the license plates checked out. Beam had it wired and on the road before he finished the Coke. On the way, he lit a joint laced with angel dust. He liked to be high when he pulled off a caper. It gave him courage.

Beam slowed at the entrance to the base and the same guard walked to the cab window.

"Surprise!" shouted Beam. He brought up his gun and blew a hole in the soldier's forehead.

He released the clutch, and the truck rolled forward on the downslope. Tons of heavy metal from the full load he was carrying smashed through the wire gate and barreled down the road.

They were waiting for him around the first curve.

He braked to slow when he saw the open ass-end of the heavy transport ahead of him. And kept going. His Army truck rolled up the ramp into the transport trailer-truck. Beam was still smoking his joint when he stopped. A truck inside a truck. Like Russian dolls. Beam smiled at his dumb joke. The angel dust was working nicely.

The back doors of the trailer closed, and the transport lurched forward even before Beam climbed down. From outside came the faint sound of explosions. The diversionary attack. Perfect timing. The lights came on in the back of the trailer. Rudy was waiting for him as he climbed down.

"Well done, Mr. Beam." Rudy's English had a heavy German accent.

Beam toked the last of the joint and flicked it out.

"Pow!" he said. "Should'a seen the blood, man! Guy's head blew open like a garden hose."

Rudy smiled generously, the way someone smiled at a naughty child. Beam continued. The combination of drugs and success made him very high.

"You know what we say in California, Rudy? We

say, 'Go with the flow.' Blood flows, he goes!'' Beam was laughing hysterically.

"I share your enthusiasm for the American soldiers' deaths," said Rudy calmly.

"Oh, man! You Germans," Beam said, shaking his head. "You guys don't get excited about nothing! Come on—get into it! We just pulled it off!"

Rudy remained calm. "We will be successful—pull it off, as you say—when we get these weapons to Marseilles. Then my job will be over."

"Yeah. Right. Marseilles." Beam calmed down. "I still got a long way to go."

"It has been a pleasure doing business with you and your...friend, Mr. Beam. It is always a pleasure to liquidate stormtroopers of American imperialism. We do our best in Europe, as you know. It has been gratifying to hear that someone is prepared to work toward our goals on another continent. Central America is so far away."

"I hear you, man." Beam nodded rapidly, not listening. He was in it for the money. "It's been great, Rudy, working with a famous terrorist and leading revolutionary like yourself, and all that. My friend is a great admirer of your organization—Direct Action, as you call it. Yeah, he's into it himself. What a joke. Hoisting weapons from the American Army so we can kill American soldiers in El Sal." Beam roared with laughter and slapped Rudy on the back. "Yeah, that's rich man, rich."

He was laughing so hard tears squeezed from his eyes. "Get ready, Central America." He brought out his gun and pretended to fire it. "*Boom!* Here we come! *Boom boom!*"

IT RAINED FOR AN HOUR before night fell. Humidity and the thick smell of tropical vegetation made the darkness impenetrable. A silent shadow stood at the edge of the clearing. His black clothing was wet from the jungle. In the glow of spotlights set along the perimeter of the wire fence, a single man stood guard, his rifle slung carelessly over his shoulder. Inside the enclosure, a long rectangle of yellow light streamed from the window of a low bungalow. Only the voices of men joking over a game of poker inside moved in the stifling heat.

The man at the edge of the forest flicked his arm over his shoulder. Immediately two more dark shapes moved out from behind him. With a barely audible shuffling they disappeared into the darkness along either side of the gate.

Their shadows fluttered along the ground like clouds falling across the moon. The guard felt a sudden hand across his mouth. For barely a second he felt the blade of a knife. The knife sliced his throat open. The lifeless body was lowered to the ground without a sound.

Men clad in black fatigues moved quickly away from the jungle. They scuttled like insects through the gate, circling away from the light of the bungalow window and disappearing into the shadows. The compound was empty again.

Laughter, cheers and a voice bragging about a winning hand exploded from the window of the bungalow.

THE DINNER PARTY WAS VERY ELEGANT. Candlelight sparkled from the cut-crystal dishes and played along the surfaces of silver trays. Major Michael Christopher caught another flirtatious glance from Nadine's warm brown eyes. The wine, conversation and the beautiful Nadine almost made Christopher forget.

He'd given up a game of poker at the compound to accept the dinner invitation from Juan de Riberas. On his way to the wealthy landowner's country estate, he thought he'd seen headlights follow his car. The lights turned off some distance before he'd arrived. But El

Salvador was a nervous and jumpy land. Sometimes it was all too easy to imagine things. Still, the weight of his Browning HP pistol under his uniform in a shoulder holster was comforting.

"A toast to the United States of America," Juan de Riberas said and held up his wineglass. "And to the assistance your country has given us in these troubled times."

Around the table, Señora de Riberas and her daughter Nadine also raised their glasses in Major Christopher's direction.

"And a toast to the success of our two countries in bringing peace to your beautiful land," Christopher seconded. He meant it, but even as he drank he knew peace in El Salvador was a long time off.

"But you must tell us, Major," asked Juan de Riberas as if reading his thoughts, "how long will it take to drive these bloodthirsty Communist guerrillas from our country? I do not know...." His arm flopped in a gesture of hopelessness. "They destroy bridges, power lines, then melt away into the hills. Last year they burned our summer house on the Gulf of Fonseca. They do not fight, only destroy, and this causes our country to be very poor."

"Our people are very concerned that El Salvador remain a free country," said Christopher. "That's why I'm here, and the other military advisors. To help train your army to fight and put the guerrillas out of business." He choose his words carefully, not adding that it would take years, possibly decades to accomplish this. "Sometimes public pressure in America makes it very difficult for our government to help countries where civil rights are abused," Christopher continued. "So it's very important that your government eliminate the death squads, too."

"Sometimes I don't think your newspaper journalists

tell the truth about our country," said Nadine de Riberas softly.

"At least," said Juan de Riberas, smiling across the dinner table at Major Christopher, "despite the terrible violence in El Salvador, we are not without islands of peace and tranquillity. Here, for example." De Riberas gestured around the luxurious dining room.

Major Christopher heard a doorbell ring faintly somewhere in the enormous villa. Through the open dining-room doors he saw a servant pass quietly to the front of the house.

Lieutenant Pete Bronsky, U.S. Army, looked across at Captain Mandrell and threw down his cards. "Two aces and a king. I don't know how you do it, Mandrell. I'm out."

Mandrell smiled broadly as he raked his winnings from the center of the table. "You can't win or lose if you don't make no bets, boys. Another hand?"

King and O'Leary threw down their cards as well. Mandrell picked them up, added them to the deck and started shuffling.

"No way I'm letting you walk out of here tonight with all that dough, Eric," said King.

Bronsky pushed himself up from his chair. "You boys have a swell evening. Playing with this guy, you'll probably put mortgages on your wives tonight." He grabbed a pack of cigarettes off the table and headed for the door.

"Where are you going?" O'Leary called, craning his neck around from the table to watch Bronsky leave.

"A quiet stroll around this enchanting compound and then to bed. We've got a busy day tomorrow."

"Yeah, the dreaded Fifty-ninth," said King, picking up his new hand and grimacing when he saw the cards. "The greenest soldiers in the El Salvador army on maneuvers. See you in the morning, Pete."

The other two soldiers threw their good-nights at Bronsky as he stepped outside and closed the door behind him. The humidity surrounded him like a soggy blanket. He pulled out a cigarette, lit it and began walking around the side of the bungalow.

Bronsky, Mandrell, King and O'Leary were four of America's eighty-odd military advisors in El Salvador. It wasn't an easy job and it wasn't much fun. In a guerrilla war there was no such thing as a draw. If you weren't winning, you were losing. And the only way to win was to go out after the enemy. Relentlessly. Without stopping, day or night.

The problem in El Salvador was that the army thought it was a nine-to-five war. Every morning soldiers would start on one of their wild-goose chases, running around after guerrillas who'd already left the region the day before. And at five o'clock it was as if they'd heard a bell ring to punch their time cards and return to barracks. It wasn't just a matter of training these soldier how to fight. Anyone could learn that. They had to be taught what war was.

It made Bronsky angry. He took another drag on his cigarette and turned the corner of the bungalow.

"Goddamn," he muttered under his breath. The gate was wide open and the guard was nowhere in sight. It wasn't the first time this had happened. He flicked his cigarette to the ground and started toward the gates.

He was halfway down the side of the bungalow when a figure in black slipped out of the shadows and stood facing him. The man held a gun. The gun was pointed at Bronsky.

"What the f—" Bronsky's curse was cut in two by the butt of a rifle that came from behind him and smashed in the side of his head. His eyes rolled upward as his body impacted against the side of the house and fell to the ground. One of the men in black bent over the crumpled body, and light flashed quickly from the blade of a knife. Bronsky stopped breathing forever.

THE CONVERSATION around the dinner table lapsed momentarily with the interruption of the doorbell.

"Now who can that be?" asked Señor de Riberas, somewhat annoyed.

Suddenly they heard a muffled scream and the sound of quickly running feet. The de Riberas family stiffened. Major Christopher stood, drawing his revolver quickly from his dinner jacket.

"Get out!" he shouted at them as the first black-suited figure reached the dining-room doors. Christopher fired once, and the man flew backward, a hole through his brain. The de Riberas family fled through another door into the back of the villa.

A second man in black appeared at the dining-room doorway, his rifle firing wildly. The shots scattered glass and dishes across the table. Christopher pulled his trigger twice, and the man collapsed onto the body of the first. There were more running steps and shouting from the hallway.

The American soldier threw himself back behind the French doors that led outside. He was standing on a long terrace that ran along the side of the villa. A third figure appeared in the dining room. Christopher ducked behind the doorframe as bullets splintered wood and shot by his forehead. He turned and fired. A scream of pain tore at the night. The villa became deathly quiet.

Major Christopher looked down the long terrace. It turned and ran around the house to the right. Halfway down, another set of open doors led into the front hallway. He began moving quietly along until he reached the edge of the doors. The hall was empty except for the two bodies sprawled at the entrance to the dining room. A trail of blood led across the carpet to the front door,

where the body of the servant lay in a lifeless heap.
Christopher crossed the doorway and moved toward the
end of the terrace.

He saw the dull gray end of a rifle poke its way
around the corner of the house and raised his gun. The
terrorist came on slowly, not seeing Christopher until it
was too late. His eyes grew wide with horror. Christopher sent a bullet through his brain. The man flapjacked
into the air, his skull exploding in a shower of blood and
bone. His rifle flew from his hands into the bushes
along the side of the terrace.

Christopher went into a roll across the open corner of
the terrace and took cover in the bushes along the
house. Bullets tore past him from somewhere near the
front door. He fired in their direction and heard a
shriek. The bullets stopped coming.

At the sidewalk, where the protective cover of the
bushes ended, Christopher could see inside the open
front doors. He smiled ruefully. An enormous gilt mirror on the far side of the hallway reflected a terrorist
flattened against the wall behind the door.

Keeping low, Christopher sped across the open sidewalk to the bushes on the other side and sent two shots
into the house. The second one spun the man back into
the room. The night was split open by a scream of pain.
The wounded man dragged himself out of sight.

Christopher raised himself to dart across the terrace
into the house when he heard the bushes behind him
crackle. He felt the cold circle of steel at the nape of his
neck.

"Drop it, pig." It was an American voice.

The rifle at the back of his head pressed harder. Then
a foot planted squarely in his back kicked him to the
ground, knocking his breath out. Another foot stepped
on his hand and began crushing the gun from his grip.

The voice snarled again.

"Now you pay."

They were the last words Major Michael Christopher heard.

INSIDE THE BUNGALOW Mandrell picked up his last card. A joker. The joker was wild. His luck was still on.

Something big hit the side of the frame building with a loud, hard thump. Three pairs of eyes met instantly across the table. Mandrell looked at King and motioned toward the door.

"Better go have a look at what Bronsky's up to."

King got up and walked to the door. He stepped out. A knife reached across the open entrance. King fell, blood bubbling down his neck and onto his chest.

Six men in black uniforms poured from the darkness into the room. Silenced rifles coughed up instant death.

O'Leary's chest exploded into gore. He flew back against the wall, his eyes stretched wide with death. Slowly he slumped to the floor, scraping a trail of blood down the wall behind him.

Mandrell dived for the window. Another rifle blasted death. Mandrell collapsed onto the sill, tearing the screen from its frame. His back was peppered red. The cards fell from his lifeless hand.

Jokers wild.

The winning streak was over.

Suffocating silence returned to the tropical night.

THE MAN SHIFTED his enormous body in the back of the stretch limousine. Few cars were big enough for his seven-foot frame. He smoothed the folds of his white suit.

Through the window he could see the lights of the capital city of San Salvador glimmering in the valley below. He waited. It was almost one o'clock. It would be over now.

Outside, three men stood with rifles held loosely in their hands, talking in low voices. The soft idle of the car and the hum of the air conditioner blocked the sounds. He waited, admiring himself for his own patience. Headlights appeared up the road. First one set, then another. A car and a van.

They were parked on the gravel road that led to the central garbage dump. For years this had been the place where the death squads had thrown the bodies of their victims. The newly elected regime had been forced by the American government to curb the death squads. The pits weren't used anymore. The vultures went hungry. But the populace was still too terrified of the area to go near it at night. It was unlikely they would be disturbed.

The two approaching vehicles slowed to a stop in front of the limo. Men clad in black got out and joined the others standing outside. One of them approached the car. The big man in the white suit rolled the window down less than an inch.

"No problems at the base, Jeremiah," said the man. "And we got the major at the de Riberas villa. But he took three with him. And three wounded. They might live if. . . ."

Jeremiah rolled up the window without listening to the rest of the sentence. There was a penalty to be paid for failure. All his soldiers knew this. All his people. And they knew what the penalty was.

He reached for the thermos on the seat beside him, pulled himself out of the seat and heaved his vast body from the car. Gravel crunched heavily underfoot as he moved toward the van.

He motioned to the men standing around.

"Dump the bodies of the Americans into the pits. Quickly!" The vultures would feast tomorrow.

Then he walked to the place where the three wounded men had been taken from the car and were resting on the side of the road. They were half conscious, their clothing soaked with blood. Jeremiah towered above them. They looked up at him, their eyes filled with pain. And with trust.

Jeremiah took three small silver cups from the pocket of his suit and filled them from the thermos.

"Drink this and your pain will be gone." His voice was low, soft and persuasive. He squatted slowly and handed the cups to two of the three wounded. The third was too weak. Jeremiah held the cup to the lips of the weak man and poured the liquid in.

The bodies of the wounded men shot straight out in instant convulsions. Their eyes bulged from their sockets, and their fists drew up to clench at the invisible monster that crushed their chests. With a terrible grating of air pushed from their lungs, they died.

Jeremiah lifted his great body slowly and turned to the other men. He made a careless gesture toward the bodies and walked back to the limo. Wordlessly the men lifted the bodies of the dead and loaded them into the van.

Back in the limo, Jeremiah carefully smoothed the folds of his suit again. A driver climbed into the front seat, and the car lurched forward along the gravel road, turning toward the east.

He watched the lights of San Salvador floating away.

Everything had gone very well. He was satisfied. Only one more operation to go.

The big one.

And Central America would be his for the taking.

2

"The senator is waiting. As usual." And as usual the blond receptionist's voice dangled icicles.

Walker Jessup didn't even bother looking her in the face anymore. He preferred the scenery in the hill country down below. He was getting to enjoy his visits to the senator's office.

The secretary aimed her long, manicured finger carefully at the intercom buzzer and pushed. Her nails looked like can openers. Jessup wondered how she could dial a telephone or hold a pencil for dictation, let alone type. But then, she didn't have to. She was hired for other reasons.

When the blonde moved, her body said yes. But the look from the blue chunks of ice that went for eyes said no.

Public relations.

Political style.

There was no such thing as a square deal in Washington.

Jessup squeezed his serious bulk into the chair in the senator's office.

The senator almost faded out of sight across the vast distance of a desk the size of a Ping-Pong table. Sitting down, he didn't have the advantage of platform shoes to boost his height. Sitting down, he looked like what he was: a little guy with a serious addiction.

The drug was power.

The senator had the market cornered.

"So. You've read the file?" The senator played with a pencil, balancing the pointed end and the eraser between his two index fingers.

Jessup nodded.

"And he's on his way?" The sharpened end of the lead pencil made a deep indentation in the senator's fingertip. The man was very tense.

"He's on his way," Jessup repeated, staring straight back.

"Excellent." The senator relaxed visibly. He put the pencil down. "And you think he'll accept. At the usual price?"

Jessup nodded. "Two hundred grand per man. Plus expenses."

"One third down, balance on completion."

"The terms are up to Nile Barrabas, the man you're hiring."

"Of course." The senator grinned.

Something was up.

Normally Jessup and the senator had a relationship of unconcealed mutual antagonism. Now the politician was sitting across his immense desk smiling at Jessup.

The senator was an architect of U.S. foreign policy. Underneath the firm, decisive public image was a power broker whose ambitions—and the favors he did for friends—sometimes got him into trouble.

And then it was time to call on Walker Jessup.

Jessup had a reputation and a nickname. The Fixer. For the right price he could fix anything. It was a tricky business. And he had a perfect track record.

He had connections in the FBI, CIA and a few other intelligence agencies where even the initials were top secret. And almost every spy, politician and diplomat in the world who threw the game for a wad of crisp American dollar bills had his number listed in Jessup's contact book.

For a long time Jessup had tried to persuade the house committee that the senator needed to finance a special-forces team, one that could operate secretly, outside the law and recognized foreign policy, settling brush fires and disturbances in various Third World countries.

The kidnapping of an African president by Kaluban terrorists had finally forced the committee to act— against the senator's persistent objections. Jessup got what he wanted. A team of men, each with his own special skill, each one totally dependable. And each one a little bit crazy.

To lead them he found an ex-Army colonel who'd done his time in Nam and earned his medals with blood. A soldier who had become sickened by the petty political intrigues that controlled the Army and had dropped out. A professional mercenary, the veteran of a dozen wars, and sought after by the leaders of private armies the world over. Jessup pulled him out of a South American prison hours before his rendezvous with a firing squad. The man's name was Nile Barrabas.

Barrabas and his soldiers were successful in the Kaluban operation. They were successful again when the Iranians built a bomb. The Soldiers of Barrabas went in, nuked Iran and made it look like an accident.

Each time, the senator had come up with an impossible mission.

Each time, the Soldiers of Barrabas had conquered and won.

Now the senator had another problem and wanted Barrabas to bail him out again.

Jessup couldn't understand why the senator was being so friendly about it. Then it came to him.

The senator had a favor to ask.

Jessup waited.

The senator stood and paced behind his desk.

"It's important, of course, that Colonel Barrabas understand the delicacy of the operation, Jessup. Our policy in Central America is containment. To keep things as they are until we have time to boost the economies there."

"And the armies of those dictators who are sympathetic to our government."

The senator raised his hands and let them fall in a gesture of helplessness.

"Sometimes stability is more important than democracy. It's a very difficult situation."

"Sure is." The truth of it was, as Jessup, the senator and everyone else in Washington knew, the U.S. had dug itself into a hole in Central America, and the problem began in Nicaragua. Instead of supporting a democratic alternative, Washington had backed the ruthless dictator Somoza. Consequently the Marxist Sandinistas had seized power, and since anything was an improvement, the people of Nicaragua supported their new government. And spread the revolution to El Salvador.

U.S. public opinion was against direct intervention in Central America. So all the U.S. could do was to give lukewarm support to the *contras* stationed in Honduras and Costa Rica who were trying to overthrow the Sandinista government. Hopefully it would give El Salvador time to defeat the guerrillas while Nicaragua was busy inside its own borders.

But the *contras* were the sacrificial lambs on the bloody altar of U.S. foreign policy. They had enough money and arms to blow up a few bridges and kill a few border guards before running back to the jungle to die of wounds and rot. Government policy—the words—said "We support you." Government policy—the money—said "Sorry, no go."

Government policy was all tits and ass and no action. Like the blond secretary in the senator's outer office.

"Jessup," the senator continued. "Whatever your opinion, our policy is the result of careful thought and planning. Unfortunately we can never take care of all the contingencies. That's why. . . ." The senator paused as if what he had to say was distasteful. It was.

"You need us," Jessup finished for him. "Yours truly. And a dirty-tricks team."

"Special forces, please," the senator corrected him. "I think we should have some respect for these men, don't you?"

"Indeed."

"And as I said, the job is delicate. Five of our military advisors in El Salvador have been brutally butchered. It could have been the death squads, or it could have been the guerrillas. All we know is that they were killed with weapons from a shipment stolen from one of our European bases a month ago. So far we've kept it from the press, but when they get hold of it you know what the result will be."

"Sure. Same old story. The hawks will scream for troops to be sent in. The doves will demand total withdrawal. And either way, American policy in Central America will melt like snow under the tropical sun."

"Exactly. Nicaragua will pour weapons into the revolutionary armies operating in El Salvador, and the *contras* in Honduras and Costa Rica will try to invade Nicaragua and we won't be able to restrain them. Nicaragua will turn around and invade Honduras and Costa Rica to get back at the *contras*. Central America will turn into a bloodbath. The Cubans will get involved."

"Then the Russians."

The senator stood with his hands on the desk and leaned over Jessup.

"There are five different armies operating in the region. One of them is behind the murders, trying to destroy American foreign policy. All we know is that a big shipment of stolen, ultramodern NATO weapons is on a ship and headed for Central America. If Barrabas doesn't eliminate the threat, America is in big trouble.''

Jessup looked up into the senator's face.

''Then why aren't you giving me all the information?''

For a moment Jessup's question caught the senator off guard. He turned away abruptly and walked back to his swivel chair and sat. When he faced Jessup again he looked angry.

''Don't push me, Jessup. Our relationship is a business relationship and arises out of necessity. We need you to solve a few problems from time to time. But without us you're out of a job. Let's be clear about that.

''You have all the information our intelligence networks have dug up. Obviously this man Beam is working with the Direct Action terrorists in Europe to foil American interests. The mission for Colonel Barrabas and his team is to eliminate Beam and the arms-importation network he has set up. And the arms, as well. In other words, to restore the balance we had established there. In the meantime, I am leaving immediately for a fact-finding tour of El Salvador, which will calm the atmosphere in Washington.''

The senator paused. He was considering something, not looking at Jessup. Jessup waited. Gut instinct told him there was more to the picture than the senator let on. And Jessup had a big gut.

''Yes?'' he prodded the senator.

''There is one further matter.'' The politician spoke slowly, not meeting Jessup's eyes. ''Since Barrabas will be infiltrating El Salvador to effect covert operations, there is a good possibility that his path and the path of the Salvadoran guerrillas will cross.''

Now Jessup knew what he was going to hear. He didn't like it already.

"This guerrilla leader Rosaria has become quite an inspiration for the revolutionaries in El Salvador. It would be of enormous benefit to us if this leader were eliminated."

Jessup finally spoke. "In other words you want Barrabas to solve your immediate problems with Beam *and* further a few foreign-policy objectives as well. All while you're down there on a fact-finding tour. How convenient." Jessup knew the senator wasn't playing any tricks. If the bottom fell out of the civil war in El Sal, it would be to his credit. And it was an election year.

"Only if the opportunity comes up," said the senator quickly. He was playing nervously with the lead pencil again. "We may as well try to get value for our money," he said weakly.

"Barrabas has been known to have a strong sense of ethics. It's one of the reasons he quit the U.S. Army after we lost Vietnam. He might get pissed off if he's asked to be an assassin."

"But you'll put it to him?"

"I'll put it to him."

"I can't see what his objections would be. He is, after all, only a mercenary. He's paid to kill."

Jessup shrugged. "Either he'll accept or he won't. Or...." Jessup didn't finished the sentence. He got up and moved toward the door. The audience was over.

"Or what?" the senator asked sharply, twirling the pencil rapidly in his fingers.

Jessup turned from the doorway and smiled.

"Or he just might come in here and eliminate you. No promises."

The senator flushed with anger. Jessup heard the pencil snap as he closed the door.

NILE BARRABAS SCANNED HIS NEWSPAPER as the Air France Concorde approached the New York coast. There was a story about an airplane that ran out of gas in midflight. The pilot managed to land safely, but it wasn't the kind of thing you liked to read about ten thousand feet up. He looked out the airplane window. The jagged skyline of Manhattan was already in view, and the plane was descending. Even from a distance New York City vibrated with movement. He folded the newspaper and watched JFK get bigger.

Barely six hours earlier he'd been having breakfast in a Paris hotel with Erika, planning the day's activities. Erika wanted to buy clothes on the rue du Faubourg St-Honoré. That evening there was the opera and, afterward, a late dinner at Julian's. Then he saw Jessup's ad in the *International Herald-Tribune*. He laid the newspaper down on the breakfast table and looked across into Erika's soft blue eyes. The room was suddenly very quiet. All she said was, "I'll help you pack."

Erika was disappointed, but she would never show it. A good woman knew enough about life with a man like Barrabas to accept his sudden departures without question.

Living fast and living hard. Never looking back or thinking about the future. Take it now, and take it all. It was the only way Nile Barrabas knew how to live. Sometimes he wondered if it was hard on Erika. But Erika was one damned fine woman.

"Are you sure you're not a movie star?" The teenage girl in the next seat interrupted his thoughts. In her lap was some lurid teen-idol magazine. It was the third time she'd asked the question since the Concorde had left Paris. Barrabas smiled.

"No, I swear. I'm just a businessman. Sorry to disappoint you."

"I dunno," the teenager said, chewing her gum

thoughtfully and flipping the pages of her magazine. "You sure look awfully familiar."

Barrabas was used to it. People looked when they saw him. Six feet four inches tall, strong chiseled features, and closely cropped almost-white hair. It was easier for them to think they'd seen him on TV or somewhere than to simply admit he was an extraordinary sight.

The Concorde taxied across the runway to the covered exit ramp, and Barrabas was quickly up and out of his seat, thankful to get his long legs moving again. His toned and muscled body moved fluidly under the gray business suit as he walked into the crowded customs area.

"Sure was sorry to drag you out of that Paris vacation," a voice drawled behind him.

Barrabas turned to look at the bulky figure of Walker Jessup standing with his hand outstretched. They shook hands.

"Jessup, I figure you get few pleasures in life greater than dragging me away from R&R."

Jessup steered him by the arm through a door on one side of the customs area and flashed his ID at a guard. The two men passed through.

"Nile, the kind of job I have, they keep giving me lots of excuses." Barrabas didn't ask who "they" were. Jessup had connections to people he didn't want to know about.

They walked quickly down a flight of stairs and out to a waiting car. Jessup had a remarkable pace for a man who indulged frequently in the pleasures of eating and spent most of his time behind a desk.

"We've got a real honey for you and your boys this time, a real honey." His tone of voice was playful, but Jessup wasn't smiling.

The two men got into the green BMW, Jessup behind

the wheel. He pulled out into the traffic streaming toward Manhattan.

"The senator offered me the limousine," Jessup said, turning to Barrabas. "I prefer this. Not as noticeable and saves gas. The senator sponsors an energy-conservation bill in the House and drives a block-long Cadillac. Well, hell, it's not my game." With one hand he began playing with the clasps of the briefcase on the seat beside him.

"That's why I'm a soldier, Jessup. It's a lot simpler. I just do my job, clean and efficient," said Barrabas. "And as secretly as possible so you guys in Washington who make all the complications can get off the hook."

"Nile, I don't call the problems. They just leave them to me to fix up after the damage has been done. And they don't make it easy. Took me years to persuade them to give me a special force. The boys on the Hill called it a dirty-tricks team until Africa. You won that one. So then they called it covert operations, and told you to nuke Iran. They were amazed you lived to tell. So now they call you a special force, Nile. You're going up in the world. Me, I prefer to call it the SOBs. The Soldiers of Barrabas. Among other things. Here, have a look at this." Jessup handed him a file from his case.

Barrabas flipped a page in the folder, his brow furrowed in concentration. Jessup turned off the exit ramp toward the Queensborough Bridge.

"The story's been held since yesterday. It'll make the papers tonight. And then—"

"There'll be hell to pay," Barrabas finished for him. "Five U.S. military advisors murdered in classic death-squad style and their bodies dumped. Death squads didn't do this, however. And neither did the guerrillas."

"That's the complication. The death squads have pretty much been put out of business. It'd be a stupid mistake for them anyway. And it's not guerrilla style."

Jessup kept one hand on the steering wheel as he aimed the BMW in a straight line across the bridge and reached into the back seat with the other. He pulled a long, heavy, aluminum case up front.

"Here's something for you to look at." He pushed it toward Barrabas.

Barrabas opened the case. Inside was an automatic rifle sealed in plastic. He didn't recognize the design. That meant it was new. Very new.

"One of the murdered soldiers, Major Christopher, took a few of his attackers with him. We don't know how many because they took the bodies, but there was a lot of blood. But someone left this behind in some bushes, along with most of his brains. The gun proves to be the big break for us."

"It's got to be German," said Barrabas. "The square design and this dull metal casing are German trademarks." He examined the firing mechanism. "There's no breech. So they've finally perfected caseless ammunition."

"You got it, Nile." Jessup knew that Barrabas knew his rifles, but his guesswork this time around was uncanny. "You're holding the G-11, the most advanced automatic rifle in the world. It's the greatest challenge in rifle technology since the invention of the automatic rifle. The Germans have solved it."

Both men knew the significance of this G-11. The problem with automatic rifles was that they fired too fast. Soldiers became weighted down with ammunition. A hundred rounds for an M-16 came to a couple of pounds. And the rates of fire were always limited by how fast the bolt could eject the spent cartridge. The solution was to design a gun that fired caseless ammunition. It had finally been done.

Barrabas held the weapon in his hands to test it for size. It felt good.

"The problem was always how to attach the explosive charge to the bullet—and not have it go off prematurely—when fed into a hot chamber. A company in West Germany figured out a chemical formula for it. Heckler and Koch are making the rifle. The bolt's job is cut in half. So they made it cylindrical, and it doubles as a firing chamber. Very simple, actually."

"And it must have an amazing rate of fire."

"Two thousand rounds a minute compared to eight hundred for an M-16. Also uses very small bullets— 4.47mm. So the recoil forces are nothing. At a hundred yards a 3-round burst is only as wide as the guy you're shooting at. Incredible accuracy. And the ammo weighs half as much as M-16 ammo. It's a beauty."

"And without the breech, it won't foul up with mud and water. The perfect merc gun."

"And the perfect guerrilla gun. It'll probably replace the AK-47 as the standard weapon in Third World wars."

"So how did this rifle end up in El Salvador?"

"Nile, we don't really know. These guns have not even finished their test trials yet and are barely out of the factory. But a load of new experimental weapons was hijacked in a terrorist attack on a U.S. military base in Germany a month ago. The theft included these rifles. And a couple of very dangerous new missiles called LANCE. It's like a cluster bomb, but it's artillery size and drops 825 little bombs scattered over individual targets. Very nasty."

Jessup dug a photograph out of his breast pocket and handed it to Barrabas.

"That's Glen Beam. Internationally renowned drug dealer and more recently involved in snuff films. You know the kind—films for perverts who like to watch women get hacked to pieces during sex. No one can pin anything on him. And we didn't know he was into arms.

But our intelligence sources indicate he was involved in the heist at Kaiserslauten and was the liaison between the Direct Action terrorists who stole the weapons and someone in Central America who's directing operations. It's not Beam. Someone else is behind this. I've known about Beam for years. Never had the pleasure of meeting him. But I do know he's not that ambitious. He likes money but not political causes. He's working for someone else, and that someone else is out to screw American policy in Central America."

"Who? Some kind of fifth column?"

Jessup shrugged. "There are already five different armies operating among three countries. Central America is a disaster waiting to happen." He looked across the seat at Nile Barrabas. "And you're going in there. We got a cable into intelligence a few days ago. A shipment of these rifles along with the LANCE missiles left Marseilles last week, mixed with agricultural machinery and destined for Mexico. The usual setup. Liberian ship called the *Sally Queen*. Enough corporate papers to stretch from here to Athens without telling us who owns it. It goes through the Panama Canal in two days."

"We follow the shipment and find who you're looking for," said Barrabas.

"And eliminate them." Jessup's voice was flat. "Is that simple enough for you, Nile?"

Barrabas was silent, his eyes straight ahead on the traffic filing into Manhattan.

"Meanwhile, I have intelligence feelers out for info on Beam, and I'll give you what I get in tonight. Other than that, the same conditions as before. You work for me, the SOBs work for you. Someone gets killed or captured, no one knows nothing. I can supply intelligence and codes, you do your own weapons."

"I have connections in Panama City."

Jessup pulled off the bridge into the frenetic East Side

traffic. The city blared at them like a loudspeaker playing heavy rock at full volume. Barrabas loved America. It was his home. But at moments like this he knew why the serenity of Europe held him for rest between wars.

"First stop is Liam O'Toole," Jessup announced, heading toward West Forty-second Street. "If he's doing today what he usually does, his blood will be half whiskey."

"He's a good soldier," said Barrabas. He stuck a cigar between his lips and lit it. "They all are. They've already won a couple of wars for you."

"Yep, that's right," drawled the Texan. "But sometimes I still don't believe those crazy sons of bitches you got working for you."

THE RUDDY-FACED RED-HAIRED MAN swallowed the double whiskey in one long gulp and deposited the glass with a loud *clunk* on the bar.

"Hit 'er again there, lad," he told the bartender. The young man grabbed the glass and filled it quickly. Liam O'Toole turned to face the goons crowding around him. Jacob Wheeler had finally caught up with him, and there was no stopping anything now.

Wheeler was Liam O'Toole's ex-boss once removed. He ran a construction company, and O'Toole had been his demolitions expert. The melon-breasted, gum-popping Thelma was Jacob Wheeler's wife. Wheeler had fired O'Toole, according to Thelma, out of jealousy for the eighteen medals he'd won for bravery. Thelma had been making eyes at O'Toole, and O'Toole had decided to take his revenge on Wheeler via Thelma's somewhat overly endowed body.

The night they'd met, Thelma was popping gum and drinking sick-looking Demon Delights. She just got on his nerves more and more. She and civilian life in general. Finally he'd picked up the second Demon Delight—rum, crème de menthe and orange bitters—and dumped it on Thelma—pineapple rings, whipped cream and all. Then he walked out.

The night hadn't been a total loss. Waiting for him in the parking lot was someone O'Toole hadn't seen in years: the man he'd served under during his stint in Vietnam, Nile Barrabas. O'Toole found his next job working for the colonel. He whipped the SOBs into shape for their first mission and went back to doing what he liked doing best: fighting wars.

Meanwhile, Thelma had gone back to Jacob Wheeler and told him that O'Toole had forced her into a certain compromising position—no fault of her own, of course. It had taken some time, but finally Wheeler had caught up with him. And he brought along a couple of goons from his construction company to help him out. The air smelled ugly. And O'Toole hadn't even got laid in the whole deal.

The bartender slid the double shakily across the bar. O'Toole downed it in one long swallow and turned back to Jacob Wheeler. Wheeler had a face like the burned-out South Bronx and the guts of a Bowery wino. O'Toole spat on the floor and flexed his arms and shoulders.

"What'll it be, Wheeler? Shall we fight one-to-one and man-to-man, or do you need the boys here to help you think it over?"

"I told you, O'Toole, you should've kept your hands off my wife. You're gonna get what's comin', foolin' with a man's wife."

O'Toole chose his words carefully. He thought he might as well have a bit of fun before the fists started flying.

"The lady told me I was doing her a wee bit of a favor, Wheeler. Seems to me she said you can't do much satisfying. Seems to me she said you can't even get it up."

Wheeler's face turned purple and the veins on his forehead stood out like ropes. O'Toole hit him.

Wheeler went down and the two goons came at O'Toole.

"So it's not to be man-to-man but man-to-animals is it, ya scum," O'Toole snarled angrily. He hit goon number one in the gut. Goon number two slugged O'Toole in the face. O'Toole hit back. Goon number one recovered, and the room smacked with the sound of fists.

O'Toole kept the two big men back but was too busy to finish off one or the other. From the corner of his eye he saw Wheeler come up with a chair in his hands. He planted a solid right into the face of one of the goons and followed it with a left to the stomach. The goon fell back gasping for air.

O'Toole went back for Wheeler just in time to see the chair pulled upward out of Wheeler's hands. Then Wheeler flew through the air and landed in a heap by the door. Before O'Toole could figure out what the hell was going on, a solid punch caught him in the side of the head.

For a moment the dim light of the bar was pricked by pinpoints of flashing white. Then he followed the punch back and connected with the face of the goon who had thrown it. O'Toole punched again. The man flew back. And another one. The man flew back some more. One more solid one now, O'Toole thought, throwing his fist forward.

Before it connected, a hand reached out, grabbed the goon by the collar and threw him through the air to crash-land in a tangle of tables and chairs. O'Toole couldn't stop his punch. He hit air, lost his balance, crashed over a table and landed on the floor.

O'Toole raised his head and saw a hand stretched down to help him up. He followed the hand up the arm and into the eyes of a tall hard man with a head of short white hair.

"I don't like it when they start to break up the furniture," said Barrabas with a broad smile.

O'Toole rose to his feet. Wheeler and company picked themselves up and made tracks for the door, leaving behind them only the last looks of fear on their faces. The bartender rose nervously from his refuge behind the bar.

"Why an' sure if it ain't the colonel sticking his nose in a man's private business again. Why, Colonel, I don't believe I'd be happier to see you if you were me own mother." O'Toole threw his arms around Barrabas in a tight Irish embrace. "Bartender! A couple of doubles to bring down the house. And do yourself a favor, lad— pour one for yourself, too."

The bartender poured a glass, downed it and with steadier hands poured two more. Barrabas and O'Toole raised their glasses.

"A toast to our very own mothers, Colonel, and a toast to long life, for them if not for us."

They drained their glasses.

"You ready to go, Liam?" Barrabas asked, setting his empty glass on the bar.

"Well, Colonel, it all depends on what you've got for me now, doesn't it." O'Toole winked.

"How 'bout a war?" Barrabas was already half out the door.

GLASS DOORS PARTED SMOOTHLY as Captain Geoff Bishop entered the inner sanctum of the airline's head office on the forty-fifth floor of a Montreal skyscraper. He sank up to his ankles in luxurious pile carpeting. Along the walls of the high-ceilinged reception area hung Inuit prints that sold for thousands of dollars on the Toronto and New York art markets. A stern, thin-lipped receptionist sat at a wide, semicircular desk that was covered with enough flashing lights, intercom receivers and closed-circuit television monitors to make it look like the control panel of the starship *Enterprise*. Behind her, two stories of plate glass looked out over downtown Montreal and the St. Lawrence Seaway. It occurred to Captain Bishop that if the airline wanted cutbacks, they could begin here in the head office instead of with maintenance crews and overtime pay. It was those cutbacks that had almost cost his life and the lives of his flight attendants and 327 passengers aboard his DC-10.

"Captain Bishop," he said, introducing himself to the receptionist. "I have an appointment here at 1400 hours."

She eyed him suspiciously through thick, horn-rimmed glasses and pursed her lips.

"Two o'clock," she corrected him in civilian time. "Mr. Carter, vice-president of employee relations, will see you shortly. Have a seat, Mr. Bishop." She pointed toward a bank of leather sofas.

"*Captain* Bishop," he corrected her.

"Yes—" the receptionist looked away with a slight smirk "—Captain."

Bishop sank into the overstuffed cushions. He didn't have a good feeling about what was about to happen.

Two weeks earlier he'd been flying his DC-10 on a regular Vancouver to Winnipeg run. Two hundred and forty miles out of Winnipeg and ten thousand feet above the green-and-gold patchwork quilt of Manitoba wheatfields, his engines failed. All of them at once. The trouble became apparent as soon as he glanced at his instrument panel. He'd run out of gas. Someone in the refueling depot in Vancouver had screwed up real good, and the plane was sinking fast.

He had one chance and that was the thin black line of

the TransCanada Highway sixty miles away, running straight as an arrow and flat as a ruler across the prairies. He knew it was there because he'd grown up in one of those dusty prairie towns ten thousand feet below. The TransCanada was the perfect runway if he could get the plane there in time. He knew the odds. They weren't good for the plane, and they were worse for any cars that happened to be traveling on that stretch of highway. But he'd probably save the lives of his passengers. Or at least he'd die trying.

He coasted the plane with the flaps down and lowered the landing gear, which slowed their descent. A few minutes later the surface of the TransCanada was coming up fast.

The plane hit the highway with a scream of wrenching metal as the wheels tore off, and the belly of the plane began to scrape away like tinfoil under the awesome friction, digging up the asphalt like a giant plow. Dozens of astonished motorists braked and veered their cars off into ditches as the DC-10 headed down the highway at them.

One driver froze at his wheel. His terror was short. The plane flattened the car as it slid down the pavement at more than a hundred miles an hour.

It was the only fatality. Other than a few minor injuries, the DC-10 passengers suffered more from shock than anything else. Captain Bishop was the hero of the morning headlines in the daily newspapers. The North American Pilots' Association was presenting him with an award.

The government announced an immediate investigation. The fuel shortage had been caused by confusion over the metric and Imperial systems of measurement. And this was compounded by a broken gauge in one tank. What the inquiry didn't reveal was the real problem. Because of airline-company cutbacks, the group of mechanics was understaffed; those working had never been trained in metric conversion.

The airline had a lot of face-saving to do over the affair. They were looking for a scapegoat, and Captain Bishop had a bad feeling it might be him. He knew company ways. He'd worked for them for the ten years since he'd left the Canadian Forces. One way or another, the little guy got screwed.

Half an hour later Bishop was still waiting. The intercom on the *Enterprise* buzzed, and the receptionist cast sly glances at Captain Bishop while secretively whispering into the receiver.

"Mr. Carter will see you now," she said, hanging up.

Carter's office was almost as big as the reception area, and another wall of glass looked out over the forests covering the slopes of Mount Royal.

"Captain Bishop, come in. Please have a seat." Carter stood and motioned toward a chrome-and-leather chair on one side of the enormous desk. Carter sat down and reclined in a high-backed swivel chair. On the desk was a leather writing pad, two pens and a small pile of neatly stacked blank paper. Bishop figured that anyone with a desk that neat didn't do much work.

"The company, as you know, views the landing of the DC-10 with the utmost seriousness," Carter began.

"So did I when I noticed the fuel tanks were empty at ten thousand feet," said Bishop. He looked straight into Carter's eyes. Carter looked away.

"Yes, quite so. And I assure you that we here at the head office are more than aware of the courage and skill you brought to bear in saving the lives of your passengers under—" Carter paused to choose the right word "—difficult conditions. Nevertheless. . . ."

Bishop knew what was coming, so he went on the offensive. "Nevertheless, if the company ensured that its maintenance crews were adequately trained in metric conversion, this wouldn't have happened. And that traveling salesman who got squashed would be home with his kids right now.''

Carter began looking uncomfortable. ''We are taking all the necessary measures to ensure that such an incident doesn't happen again. As you know, our company has the finest safety record in the world. However—and despite your admirable actions—we cannot overlook your responsibility in the matter.''

Bishop looked steadily at Carter. Carter swiveled his chair around to stare out at Mount Royal and avoid Bishop's eyes.

''My responsibility,'' said Bishop flatly.

''In not ensuring that the DC-10 was adequately fueled,'' said Carter. Bishop waited. Carter continued. ''I very much regret being the one to tell you. But we have decided to put you on a one-year suspension without pay.''

''One-year suspension, eh?'' Bishop stood up, leaned over the desk and grabbed Carter by his white collar and silk tie.

''Look at me, you bastard!'' Bishop commanded. Carter's eyes grew wide with fear, his mouth gasped for air, and chubby fingers began pulling at Bishop's steel grip. ''I'll do you one better.'' Bishop pushed him back into the chair. The high back bobbed back and forth, and Carter bobbed up and down like a jack-in-the-box.

''This is a serious matter, Captain Bishop,'' Carter sputtered.

Bishop grabbed a blank sheet of paper off the top of the neatly stacked pile and a gold pen from the leather writing pad. He scribbled quickly, signed it and shoved it into Carter's face. Carter's fearful eyes flicked over the writing. There were two words: ''I quit.''

''Now stick it where the moon don't shine,'' said Bishop, using an expression he'd picked up during his prairie boyhood. ''And if you big-city fellows can't figure that one out, it means up yours.''

Carter was still spluttering when Bishop left. ''You'll be blacklisted for this! You'll never work again!'' Bishop gave him the finger.

As the ex-pilot walked across the broad plaza at the foot of the skyscraper, he stopped to toss his captain's hat into a nearby trash barrel. Then he stood on the corner of the busy street, trying to figure out what to do next. He knew it wasn't just Vice-President Carter and the other idiots on the forty-fifth floor. It was the whole bloody business.

Geoff Bishop lost his parents when he was sixteen, and there wasn't a lot to do hanging around the wheat silos in dusty prairie towns. So he joined the army, transferred to the air force, and moved his way up to officer and pilot. He learned everything he could about helicopters, transports and bombers. Then he was sent with the Canadian contingent of the U.N. peace-keeping force to the Suez, and after Nasser kicked them out in 1967, he went to Cyprus. He picked up a few decorations along the way and became a bit of a hero for evacuating a Greek-Cypriot village under terrorist attack while taking two bullets in his back and side. He could never understand all the fuss about it. To him it was just a job.

He couldn't understand it either when his wife wanted him to give up the military and settle down for a quiet life. But he did. After a couple of years of civilian flying, taking winter vacationers to Florida condos and summer travelers to gawk around Europe, he was bored. But he did make damned good money. Then, having left the air force for his wife, she left him because she still didn't like his absences. So now he paid most of what he earned in alimony.

All in all, his prospects weren't good. He'd be broke

for the rest of his life. He might find a job piloting a Twin Otter around the mining towns of northern Ontario. If he was lucky.

It was a bleak future. So bleak he didn't notice the car pulling to a stop at the curb in front of him. Or the tall, white-haired man who got out and approached him.

"Captain Geoff Bishop?" The stranger extended a hand, which Bishop shook. "I understand you might be looking for work," the man continued.

"How did you. . . ." Bishop knew the word would get out fast, but this fast?

"Let's talk about it in the car." There was something about this man's voice that Bishop recognized from his air force days. It was a voice used to commanding.

They got into the back seat. A man with bright red hair pulled the car out into the traffic and turned toward the freeway along the St. Lawrence River.

The man had a file in his lap.

"You had a good military career. You left it for civvies. Now you have no career at all." The white-haired man was smiling. Bishop couldn't help giving a small laugh.

"Right. Now how the hell do you know about all this?"

"And no money."

"And no money."

"What kind of shape are you in? Physically."

"I work out every day. Ski. Swim. And lacrosse."

"Your marksmanship's still good?"

"I keep it up at the Canadian Riflemen's Club. Handguns." Bishop paused. He liked this man, whoever he was. But could he trust him? He thought so. "I have my own collection up at my house in the country."

"Have you given much thought to your future?"

Bishop laughed again. "You haven't given me any time."

"Name's Barrabas. Nile Barrabas. Formerly a colonel in the U.S. Army. Now I'm involved in other projects." He handed Bishop an airplane ticket. "That flight leaves for Miami in an hour."

The man in the front seat looked at them in the rearview mirror.

"Dorval?" he asked.

Barrabas nodded to Liam O'Toole. "Dorval." The car headed for the airport. He turned back to Bishop. "If you don't mind dropping out of sight for a while, I have an offer I think will interest you."

3

Jessup swore when he saw the line. Three hundred people talking Midwestern snaked through the marble Art Deco lobby of the Empire State Building.

There was one elevator.

He bought a ticket and waited. Half an hour later he arrived at the observation level. It was wall-to-wall tourists. King Kong dolls of every imaginable size hung everywhere, with price tags as ridiculous as their acrylic fur. The bigger ones reminded Jessup of his own bulk. He made a mental note to go on a diet.

Then he changed his mind as he used his body as a battering ram to get through the crowd. No one noticed him shoving through. They were too absorbed in buying King Kongs.

The man he was meeting was outside, gazing through the wire and bars put up to stop the jumpers. He wore jeans and a heavy plaid shirt.

Jessup maintained his own elaborate intelligence network. He was a switchboard of information. It was a big advantage in a private operation. There was no one to tell him what he couldn't do, who he couldn't talk to. And people loved to talk. Usually for money.

But not in this case.

His long experience inside the official and unofficial agencies had left him with a long list of friends. The big Texan commanded their loyalty because they trusted him. They were hamstrung by the rules laid down by Congresses and administrations who didn't understand the cutthroat world of intelligence collection. And when they were up against something serious, they knew they could rely on Jessup for a word in the right ear.

The Fixer's reputation went a long way.

"Incredible city," Jessup said, squeezing in beside his friend. The canyoned streets of Manhattan stretched in even rows far and wide. From below the noise from the rivers of traffic sounded like the roar of a distant waterfall.

"What kept you?" the man asked.

"The line. Helluva place for a meeting."

Both men kept their eyes looking out over the city like two strangers new in town and seeing the sights.

"We're lost in the crowd here. I figured with all these King Kong dolls no one would notice a big guy like you."

"Funny boy. Got something for me?" Jessup was smiling. He felt a faint pressure against the side of his long coat, and his pocket felt heavier.

"Those are the codes you asked for."

"Any other news?"

"It's hot. Very hot. Too hot to handle for certain friends of ours."

Jessup gave a barely perceptible nod. Some kids playing tag around the observation deck ran by screaming, and one of them bashed into Jessup. He swore. People had a habit of bumping into him. Again he made a note to go on a diet.

His friend was shuffling slowly through a handful of glossy New York postcards. Jessup watched carefully from the corner of his eye. The man stopped briefly at one picture. The picture of an enormous man.

A man who really was the size of King Kong. Without the fur.

Jessup's friend shuffled on to more postcard pictures of the Big Apple.

"Who is it?" Jessup asked, staring far ahead at the two skyward fingers of the World Trade Center.

"Calls himself Jeremiah. As in the Bible. Prophet of doom. He was busy back in San Francisco in the hippie days. Started a thing called New Society and talked a lot about utopia. People listened. He's charismatic."

"And a giant."

"Yup. For real. Seven feet tall. A head the size of a medicine ball and hands like tennis rackets. He acquired followers. And money. Ten years ago he moved everyone to a chunk of land in Honduras. They're building a New Society there. That's what they call their settlement, too."

"And what goes on there?"

"The million-dollar question, pal. He's got over a thousand people. Mostly they work at farming and crafts. What Jeremiah says, goes. But after that, no one knows anything for sure."

"Your organization hasn't penetrated it?"

The man shook his head. "We sent a man in two years ago for a look. We were never able to infiltrate."

"Dead?"

The man shook his head. "Joined up."

Jessup gave a low whistle. "Very charismatic. The connection is what?"

"The highest and the lowest. Beam, for example."

Jessup waited.

"Nothing for sure. Like everything else about Jeremiah. But we do know that he and Beam had some connections back in San Francisco. Beam was involved in hard-drugs manufacturing and sales. We think he supplied drugs to Jeremiah. And Jeremiah may have supplied women for Beam's snuff films."

"And what does Jeremiah need drugs for?"

"Instant charisma. Just add persuasion."

"Brainwashing."

The man nodded. "We think," he added forcefully.

"So maybe they still have a connection going. Beam and Jeremiah."

"Maybe. But you're missing it, Jessup."

"Uh-uh." Jessup shook his head. "The other connections."

The informer went on.

"Jeremiah got a lot of credit in Frisco back when he started. You know, daring social experiments, helping the poor, the underprivileged. Made a lot in government grants and even more in donations from rich people who felt guilty about all the money they spent on cocaine and dames. When he moved south he left behind an organization to take care of business and keep the money coming in. Even now. Even from the government now. And as we all know, the government doesn't have any money these days."

"So how does he do it?"

The man named a certain senator in Washington. The senator with the blond secretary. Jessup felt as if a piece of a puzzle had just fallen into place.

"Heavy duty."

"Mmm-hmm. And our agency got a hands-off notice after we sent our agent down there. So we can't touch it."

There was a long silence between the two men.

"Thanks," Jessup said.

"S'all right, pal. You owe me one."

The man shoved his pile of postcards into Jessup's hands and moved away from the rail into the souvenir booth where he bought a giant King Kong doll. Jessup watched him disappear. He was a brave man. He was risking his life.

Jessup thought about it a long time before heading for the elevator.

FROM HIS VANTAGE POINT at the top of the tuna tower, thirty-four feet above the deck of the tournament cruiser, Claude Hayes spotted the swordfish and the helicopter at roughly the same time. The helicopter was flying from the Florida coast in their direction, still a tiny dot about five miles off. The swordfish was lazing in the sun just under the surface of the water about three hundred feet off the port side. It was the biggest one Hayes had ever seen. He forgot about the helicopter.

"Hey, boys, we got ourselves a fish!" he shouted down to Emilio Lopez who was steering the cruiser from the bridge. He scrambled down to join Alex Nanos and today's customer, Mr. Thompkins, in the cockpit. Thompkins already had himself in the rotating chair, his feet up for leverage, looking like the commander of a battleship. It was obvious the guy didn't know what he was doing.

"Well, it's about time!" Thompkins bitched. "After all that money I paid, I'd just about given up on you fellows. Now you just sit back and let me reel it in."

Hayes's eyes locked with Alex Nanos's, who looked apologetic. He was the one who'd gotten them into this.

"Well, if you need a little hand there, Mr. Thompkins, Alex will be glad to help you out," said Hayes. "I'm just the hired hand." Nanos winced. Hayes headed for the bridge.

Claude Hayes, Alex Nanos and Emilio Lopez made an unlikely trio. Each came from a different background and life-style until a professional mercenary and ex-Army colonel named Nile Barrabas had come along and offered them the edge that each had been waiting for.

Claude Hayes came from a family of black intellectuals in Detroit. He had gone from college to civil-rights activist to a one-man rampage of destruction when Martin Luther King, Jr., died from an assassin's bullet. He escaped from his Southern prison and the two years he spent on a chain gang, acquired a new identity and joined the Navy. Diver training and expertise in underwater demolition seemed to give Hayes the peace of mind he sought, as well as a chestful of medals. But Hayes had a problem. As soon as the boss felt he was doing a good job, Hayes felt he was doing something wrong. He quit. And reappeared in Africa fighting against the Portuguese in the guerrilla wars. The Portuguese lost and the wars were over. The promise of a high position in the government of a new African country didn't appeal to him. It was the kind of thing he'd been running from all his life. So Hayes shouldered his knapsack—the sum total of his worldly possessions—and moved to Nigeria. In Lagos he opened up a charter and deep-sea fishing business. That was where Colonel Barrabas tracked him down. Hayes closed up shop and went back to war.

Nanos and Lopez couldn't have been more different. They both had distinguished careers in the Coast Guard that had resulted in each of them winning medals for bravery and ouster for breaking too many rules.

Nanos could sail anything that floated, but the Coast Guard had too many rules and not enough room for the finest navigator who'd ever served them. Lopez had worked his way out of a career as a forger with a Puerto Rican street gang on Manhattan's Lower East Side, to the command of his own Coast Guard cutter. Then it was discovered that he'd been using his ship to pick up marijuana shipments in international waters.

When Nile Barrabas found them, Nanos was making a living as a gigolo and Lopez was in for fifteen at Yarmouth federal penitentiary. Both of them brought their special expertise to the SOBs. In return, the SOBs gave them a new lease on life.

It was when they were off duty and waiting for another war that life got stale again.

They made good money as mercs. Very good money. It bought a lot of booze, a lot of women and a lot of good times. But it couldn't stave off routine.

Nanos especially began to lose his discipline when he was out of action. He knew it made a difference when he went back to fighting. The difference between winning or losing. Between life or death.

One night he, Lopez and Claude Hayes polished off a few bottles of Scotch. Hayes entertained them with stories about the pleasures of the deep-sea fishing he'd done in the waters off the Nigerian coast. If Hayes and the bottle of whisky were to be believed, the fish he caught challenged the *Guinness Book of Records* as well as the limits of biological possibility.

But it was something else that impressed Nanos. Hayes talked about the teamwork and precise timing needed to haul in a prizewinner. Most anglers didn't like to hear it, but eighty percent of the credit for a catch goes to the crew. It sounded like a great way to stay in condition between wars.

The next day, Nanos and Lopez went out and paid cash for the finest sixty-foot cruiser to be found in the waters of the Florida coast. And set themselves up in business.

A lot of wealthy sportsmen came to these waters in search of sailfish, swordfish and marlin. Nanos and Lopez could pick and choose their customers. And when they heard from the colonel, they just closed up shop for the duration.

It seemed like a great idea at the time. The only problem was that although both men were expert sailors, neither knew the first thing about catching fish.

Since his stories had given the two wild men the idea, Claude Hayes felt responsible. Besides, he reasoned, he couldn't abandon the two men with whom he'd just been through war. It would be like walking out on brothers. So the black man stayed around to show them the ropes.

All had gone well. The three of them were having a ball. Until the day temptation struck and Nanos went back to his old habits.

The handsome Greek spotted a real catch, in this case two blondes cruising the marina in Palm Beach. The ladies wanted to rent the boat for a day of deep-sea fishing. Nanos hoped the staterooms might see more use than the outriggers. That morning, bright and early, the ladies showed up with their "uncle," Mr. Thompkins, in tow. Thompkins went out in the boat demanding they find him a prizewinning fish, while the two blondes stayed on shore waving goodbye from the pier.

In the cockpit, Nanos heard the unmistakable tapping sound of the swordfish taking the bait into its birdlike beak. The strike pulled the line from the outrigger, giving the fish slack to take the bait undisturbed.

"We got a strike!" Nanos yelled to the bridge. He looked at Thompkins in the chair. He was reeling in the line. Nanos grabbed the gear release and the line spun out madly.

"Wait until the hook's set. The fish isn't going to take the bait if you're pulling it away from him."

On the bridge, Lopez rammed the cruiser into neutral so the bait wouldn't be pulled from the fish's mouth. He looked at Hayes.

"Should've used him for bait," Lopez said, jerking his head in the direction of their customer.

"Fish wouldn't have gone for it," said Hayes. "Guys like that think deep-sea fishing means frozen, ready-fried fillets jumping out of the waves onto the nonslip decks all by themselves. He'll blow it and tell us we didn't know what we were doing."

"Too bad we're wasting it on him."

Hayes nodded in agreement. The swordfish was nature's submarine, the fastest swimming fish alive, a combination U-boat and torpedo with its streamlined-for-speed body and a spear that had been known to penetrate six inches of hardwood and even copper plate. He regretted as much as Lopez that this guy had it on the line. It deserved a better opponent.

The swordfish, suddenly aware that it had been hooked, started to fight back, chasing away from the boat. Lopez steered around to give chase. In its final, frantic efforts to throw the lure, the swordfish jumped.

For Claude Hayes it was one of the most incredible sights known to man. The fish rocketed up from the blue sea in a rush of white water, its purple skin dazzling in the sunlight, its jaws open and the great arc of its dorsal fin stretched wide along its back. The deadly spear waved from side to side as the fish tried to drop the hook. For a brief moment at the height of its arch it seemed to walk along the surface of the ocean with its tail. Then it plunged back into the waters.

"Take up the slack, man, or you'll lose it!" Nanos shouted at Thompkins.

"Just let me handle this my way, boy."

It was the word "boy" that did it. Nanos grabbed Thompkins by the collar, picked him up and set him on the deck. Thompkins opened his mouth to protest. The words died on the man's tongue when he saw the look on Nanos's face. Nanos took the chair and reeled while Lopez gunned the boat forward to tighten the line. Then Hayes heard the sound of rapidly thumping air. He remembered the helicopter.

Nanos and Lopez saw it at the same time. The bird was rushing in on the cruiser from ninety degrees off the port side. Lopez kept his angle to the tiring fish as the helicopter came fast and low over the boat, barely swerving to miss the tuna tower.

"Holy shit." Hayes felt himself ducking his head

even under the cover of the bridge. He dived for the Colt they kept stored under the control panel. The helicopter turned and started back on a wild angle without breaking speed.

"Lopez, keep this mother on course! I'm bringing this in!" Nanos yelled up at them. Thompkins stood by the chair frozen in panic, his eyes fixed on the helicopter making its return to sweep across the boat again.

Hayes took the Colt in his hand and watched the helicopter come in. He couldn't see guns, but he could see two men inside behind the glass. The helicopter ran in over the boat, pulled up short on the other side, did a hairpin turn, slowed and came back to float above the deck of the cruiser. The whirling air slammed down, flattening Hayes's upturned face. Suddenly he dropped the gun and started laughing.

"Man, you wanna tell me what's going on?" Lopez demanded, still steering the boat thirty degrees off the fish with one hand and watching Nanos and the copter at the same time. A head topped with bright red hair appeared at the door of the bird, and a rope ladder dropped.

"I don't know who the hell's driving that bird," said Hayes, still laughing, "but that's Liam O'Toole trying to scare the shit out of us."

"It's sounded!" Nanos called to the bridge, his concentration still on the fighting swordfish. Lopez put the cruiser in neutral. O'Toole was clambering sideways down the ladder. Hayes and Lopez could see the pilot above them, waving behind the glass bubble. O'Toole pushed off a few feet above the cockpit and landed on the deck. The helicopter pulled up and headed for shore.

"That's the new guy," said O'Toole, waving a thumbs-up at the disappearing aircraft. "Brought me out so I could try me a bit of fishing. Looks as if I'm late for the catch."

"You ugly Irishman! You just about got the wrong kind of welcome." Hayes showed him the gun in his hand.

"Man, I was about to jump ship and swim for Cuba," Lopez called from the bridge.

In the cockpit Thompkins started to sputter, demanding answers and his money back.

"Well, bring in the fish, boys, and make it quick. The colonel wants us in Panama tonight."

Ten minutes later, with Lopez gently reversing and Nanos still in the chair reeling, they had the swordfish off the side of the boat.

"Prizewinner for sure," Nanos said, looking down at it in the water. He held the leader tight in his gloved hand.

"Bring that on up here, boys. That's going on the wall in my den." Thompkins was jumping about excitedly, his earlier anger forgotten. Nanos and Hayes exchanged glances.

Hayes held a long harpoon into the water and up against the dorsal fin. He drew back a lever, and with a snap the water bubbled and the enormous fish shuddered. Nanos cut the leader with pliers. The fish fell back into the water, momentarily stunned, then sank slowly to the depths.

"My fish!" Thompkins roared.

"Tagged it," Hayes said with a smile.

"One swordfish to live and fight another day," said Nanos.

"Hold on, boys," O'Toole yelled from the bridge. Lopez gunned it. The cruiser jerked forward. Thompkins slid against the side of the boat and would have plunged into the water if Nanos hadn't grabbed him.

"Forgot to tell you," Nanos explained. "We're in a hurry. We got a hot date waiting for us on shore."

DUSK IN NEW YORK CITY BEGAN to sparkle as the lights came on, running up the rock walls of the skyscraper canyons, struggling along the crowded streets and avenues.

Times Square relaxed into the evening and the pleasures that came with nights of cheap perfume. Overhead the giant advertising billboards blared their messages. Yellow taxis rushed past, taking their loads to the theater. Black and Puerto Rican teenagers sauntered by, carrying ghetto blasters the size of pianos on their shoulders.

Barrabas stood on a corner and watched it, breathed it all in. He glanced at his watch. He had about five minutes to enjoy it, so he put the war on hold. For a brief moment, he felt a rush of love for America. America had everything, and on the streets in front of him he could see it all.

From corporate directors watching TV in the backs of their limos to blind beggars selling pencils. From prostitutes of every sex to cops with diamond studs in their ears. Some things even made Barrabas wonder. But Times Square was one of the few places where no one gave a tall, hard man in jeans and a black leather jacket a second look.

He bought two hot dogs at a fast food outlet. New Yorkers never ate the dogs and usually drew back in disgust at the suggestion of it. But it was a tradition of his and had been since he'd run away from Wyoming at seventeen, got off the bus at the Port Authority terminal, bought a hot dog with his last fifty cents in Times Square and walked across the street to the Army recruiting office. He lied about his age to join up.

The recruiting office was still there and so was the line. He watched the young men, some hardly more than boys, standing silently in the line, their faces brave, their eyes a little lost, a little confused but filled with hope.

Hope.

America's future stood in line in the center of Times Square.

Young men who believed in their country. Believed enough to die for it.

Barrabas had believed once, too.

He didn't know any of them from Adam, but they still made him proud. He wished them luck.

The green BMW drew up to the curb beside him. The war was back on-line.

Barrabas opened the door and slid into the seat beside Jessup.

"Dinner?" He shoved the hot dog into Jessup's big paw. Jessup looked at it with disgust. He loved food, but hot dogs were a bit out of his class. He chomped.

"Not bad. Not bad at all," he said, chewing.

He pulled out into the right lane and immediately got locked in jammed-up traffic.

"When you get out of here, you can drop me at the airport," said Barrabas.

"You got everyone rounded up?"

Barrabas went down the list. "O'Toole should have Lopez, Hayes and Nanos landing at the Panama City airport right about now. Starfoot and Nate Beck have been hiding out in New York and are waiting for me at JFK. And Lee Hatton's coming in from Majorca in an hour. Our plane leaves in two. I found an airman this afternoon." He briefed Jessup on the Canadian pilot.

A man with wild eyes ran into the street and screamed in Jessup's window something about burning in a lake of fire and the end of the world. Jessup threw the rest of his hot dog at him and rolled up the window. He pulled the car around the corner and pushed it fast down Forty-eighth Street toward the East River.

"I'll fill you in on what I got, Nile." He handed Barrabas a thick envelope. "Those are the communications codes and maps you need. But check out the photograph inside."

Barrabas found the picture of Jeremiah and studied it.

Jessup briefed him on the man's history.

"The connection's not positive, but Beam apparently did business with Jeremiah some years ago in California."

"So that might be our fifth column."

"Might be. Which means you'll be going into Honduras, probably via El Salvador. But you'll have to follow the arms aboard that ship to make sure. And wipe out the support system." Jessup paused. Barrabas waited.

"There's a problem. Jeremiah is very well connected. To the press and to certain political elements in the country."

"In Washington?"

"In Washington," Jessup confirmed. He didn't mention the senator.

"So you're saying this job has to be done delicately."

"Very delicately. Like try not to leave a lot of bodies lying around. And get out fast when you've finished."

The lights of New York faded behind them as Jessup turned the car toward JFK.

Jessup continued.

"The area of southwestern El Salvador you'll be going through is guerrilla controlled, commanded by a very famous guerrilla warrior named Rosaria."

"Rosaria? Pansy name for a guerrilla hero."

"Not hero, Nile. Heroine. Rosaria's a woman." Jessup looked sideways at Barrabas. The highway lights outside silhouetted a hard, determined profile.

"I'll be damned."

"Surprised?"

"A little. But since Lee Hatton joined the SOBs, I've learned that a woman can fight a war as well as a man."

"There's another problem. Radio Venceremos, the guerrilla radio station based in Managua, announced a few days ago that any American mercenaries found in El Salvador will be shot on sight. Could be difficult if you crossed paths with the guerrillas."

Walker Jessup stopped talking and waited.

"Jessup, what are you setting me up for?"

"Nothing, Nile. I'm just saying it could be difficult— unless you were to eliminate Rosaria before she had a chance to eliminate you."

He looked at Barrabas again. The colonel kept his eyes on the highway ahead, his face expressionless, not revealing the hot anger that blasted through his blood.

"I see what you're getting at, Jessup." The soldier kept his voice even. "You desk-job guys have a problem in Central America and you're sending me in to solve it. Since I'll be in the neighborhood, you want me to knock off a few people I might run into along the way. No extra cost, and it sure would help in America's losing battle down there."

Jessup shrugged. "I'm just putting it to you, Nile."

"Jessup, I spent a lot of time in Central America with the Army and as a merc. Those people down there are crushed under some of the cruelest dictatorships I've ever seen. They rebel, and the U.S.A. chooses the wrong side every time. It's not bad luck. It's just stupid!"

"What's this? The old Nile Barrabas I knew in Vietnam full of ideas about fighting the right kind of war?"

"Uh-uh. That guy you knew in Vietnam is dead. He died on the roof of the American Embassy when the last chopper shoved off with me hanging on to the sled."

"So you want out?"

"No. You gave it to me. I'll do it. But I'll do it my

way. If those bastards in Washington want me to knock off a few guerrillas along the way, it'll cost. It's a separate deal with a separate bill. That's all."

"Fair enough, Nile. Just asking."

They rode in silence until the JFK terminals came into view. As Barrabas left the car he turned back to the Fixer.

"You've been behind a desk too long, Jessup. Get back into the trenches for a while. See what it's like." He slammed the door and walked toward the terminal entrance.

"I'M SORRY, MR. PORTER, I can understand your problem, but there's absolutely no way we can delay Flight 572 to Panama until the connection from Madrid arrives. I'm sure you can understand our position."

The airline company manager was apologetic but unmovable. Mr. Porter gave a curt nod and a thank-you, then walked to the cushioned benches where his two colleagues were waiting.

"There's no way they're going to hold it for us," said Barrabas. "We'll have to fly to Panama without her."

Nate Beck drummed the leather of the large suitcase he held. Beside him sat Billy Starfoot II, "Billy Two" as he was known in the SOBs.

Most of them had already gone on to Panama. Barrabas, Beck and Billy Two were due out on the next plane from JFK, along with Lee Hatton. But Lee was flying in from Madrid, the plane was late, and she was going to miss the connection to Panama.

From the beginning, Lee Hatton had been an unexpected addition to the SOBs. Jessup had manipulated Barrabas into taking her along. The African hostage they had been sent to rescue in Kaluba had had severe medical problems. Hatton was a doctor. She was also a skilled intelligence agent, an expert in the martial arts and a damned fine soldier. She was indispensable, and none of them liked the idea of leaving her behind.

"Give us a small, medium or economy-size war to fight and it's no problem," said Billy Two. "But battling a bureaucracy is another thing altogether."

Barrabas nodded. That was the problem with working as a special force outside official channels. They had no pull.

Nate Beck stood up, shifting his suitcase to the floor. It was heavier than it looked. It contained a computer.

"Colonel, give me twenty minutes. There's more than one way to delay an airplane." He motioned toward the arrival-and-departure readout screens overhead. "Airline computers are a cinch to plug into."

Nate Beck was a computer wizard, a genius with electronics. The codes he developed during his stint in the Air Force were ripped off by intelligence agencies and were still in use. Private industry had been a snap, and Beck rose quickly to the top of his field. And there were no more challenges. He decided to steal a million dollars. He tapped into bank accounts with his computer and skimmed the nickels and dimes out of thousands of accounts. Then his wife turned him in.

Barrabas caught up with him in a Swiss hotel room about ten minutes before Interpol showed. Nate Beck, a nice Jewish boy from Queens with a 170 IQ, was only too glad to accept a new job and a new identity. When he wasn't living computers, he was living in his own Errol Flynn fantasy world of heroes and adventure. Barrabas offered him the fantasy for real.

Now Nate Beck felt he was born to the trench coat he wore belted with the collar turned up.

Barrabas watched his man disappear down the long terminal corridor. He didn't know what Beck was up to, but if anyone could temporarily sabotage airport computers, it was he.

"C'mon, I'll buy you some coffee," Barrabas said to Billy Two. They began walking toward the stand-up bar. Airports were the last place in the world where Barrabas liked to spend time. It was like putting his life on hold. Barrabas liked to move.

"Hey, get a look at these," said Billy Two. He stopped at a magazine rack outside the airport bookstore. Neither of them noticed how many curious people glanced at them.

Billy Two was a full-blooded Navajo Indian. He was also about the size of a grizzly bear. Like the other SOBs, Billy Two had an Army career during which he became an expert in guerrilla warfare, survival training, parachuting, mapping and the martial arts. And like the other SOBs, he was an outsider.

Barrabas looked at what Billy Two had pointed at. A rack filled with men-at-war magazines. He picked one out and flipped through it. "The glamorous life of the mercenary," said Barrabas softly.

Billy Two gave a small laugh. "Action, adventure, excitement and see the world."

Full-color pictures of clean, healthy soldiers standing in tropical landscapes with colorful natives glared from the pages along with advertisements and articles on exotic weaponry and warfare techniques.

"They never write about the excitement of standing around airports or being holed up inside too many hotel rooms waiting for the word," said Barrabas, shaking his head.

"Or about the other thing," said Billy Two.

Barrabas knew what Billy Two meant. Putting your life or the lives of your men on the line. The look in a dying man's eyes. The simplest rule of all: kill or be killed.

"Who was it who said warfare was total boredom alternating with minutes of pure terror?" asked Billy Two.

"Every soldier who ever fought a war and saw the dark side of human nature," said Barrabas. "I wouldn't have any other kind of life. You and the rest of the SOBs wouldn't, either. But we pay for it. A lot." His thoughts flashed back to Erika standing in the hotel room in Paris, watching him go.

Barrabas and Billy Two leaned against the snack bar's counter drinking bad coffee and waiting once again. Through the glass wall of the snack bar, Barrabas stared down the long corridor of the terminal deep in thought. Then it happened.

The arrival-and-departure readout screens suspended from the ceiling down the long length of the terminal suddenly shimmered and one by one went black. Groups of travelers standing below fell into shocked silence, waiting for the screens to come back on. They didn't. Traffic in the terminal came to a halt. Then the low murmur of alarm swelled to a hubbub of panic. Barrabas nudged Billy Two. A reassuring loudspeaker announced a temporary malfunction. Nate Beck appeared at Barrabas's side, carrying his suitcase.

"Minor difficulties." He grinned. "It won't affect air-traffic control, but the twenty minutes it takes them to get their readouts back in order should result in about a two-hour traffic jam on the runways."

Barrabas clapped Beck on the back, and three smiling soldiers walked through the terminal.

Just as the screens went back on twenty minutes later, the tall, aristocratic woman with short brown hair and dark eyes walked through the customs exit.

"Hello, Colonel." She had a big smile and a low, sultry voice. Barrabas moved forward and they shook hands.

"Glad to know you still need a doctor on your missions," she said.

Barrabas shook his head.

"Lee, the first time I had no choice. Jessup forced me to take you along."

"But Jessup has nothing to do with it anymore, Colonel. The last few assignments, it's been completely up to you. I'm. . . I'm honored, you know."

Barrabas took her by the arm, and they began walking toward the departure lounge. Before he'd seen Lee Hatton in action he never thought of fighting as anything other than a man's job. But Hatton had not only kept up with the men. She'd been accepted by them as an equal.

"You've earned your ticket, Lee. You're a damned fine soldier. As well as a damned fine doctor. But this time we may have need of some of your other talents as well.

"We're going into Central America. Depending on our luck, we could have any one of five different armies on our tail. Or all of them at once. This could turn into the war of all against all."

Barrabas stopped and looked at her. She was a beautiful woman. And he knew that as much as he admired her, and despite the many times he'd seen her in action, he still wasn't totally used to the idea of women warriors.

"You've got a background in diplomacy. Considering where we're going, if we run out of firepower, we may need a negotiator. You never know." He meant it as a joke, not a prophecy.

Barrabas put his arm around her shoulders in a gesture of comradeship. "It sure as hell isn't one of my skills," he concluded. "Come on, we've got a plane to catch."

4

Barrabas gazed out over the rooftops of Colón through the high plate-glass windows of the hotel conference room.

Across Limón Bay dual breakwaters stretched like long thin arms to protect the bay from the squalls and hurricanes that blew in from the North Atlantic each year. Beyond, the indigo waters of the Caribbean were calm and inviting under the hot sun.

And shark infested.

That was the razor's edge of this tropical paradise. Under the surface lurked savagery. The relentless struggle for power among men.

Barrabas knew. He had spent a lot of time in Central America. On business. And he knew there'd be a need here for men of his profession for many years to come.

"Colonel, I don't know where you got these codes from, but they work. It's fantastic—I'm in!" Beck was as excited as a little kid with a new Christmas toy when he started playing with his computers. This time he was plugging into the computers of the Panama Canal Company.

Barrabas leaned over the wizard's shoulder. A series of one-syllable nonsense words ran across the screen.

"It's military. The Panama Canal is one of America's most strategic assets. The Panama Canal Company controls the canal and the Zone, and the sole shareholder is the Secretary of the U.S. Army."

"I could have figured them out myself. It would have taken a lot longer, though," said Beck.

"When will you have the information?"

"Well, now that I'm in, I have to locate the correct files, then cross-check them with other possibilities and get readouts. I should have something in a few minutes. It'll take a few hours to check the whole schedule."

Barrabas looked at his watch. It was almost 1100 hours. They were losing time. In small groups, the SOBs had flown into Panama the night before, registering as salesmen with DataRand Corporation, a computer company specializing in software. It gave them the perfect cover to take over one of the hotel's penthouse conference rooms as an urban "field" headquarters. While the others crashed out for a few hours, Lopez set up a portable light board and began forging PCC identification papers. Beck went to work with the computer.

In a few hours Barrabas would have the complete scheduling for Panama Canal traffic. He'd know when the *Sally Queen* was going through, how long it would take and when it sailed from Balboa on the Pacific side. He had some extra cargo to load on board. Three of the SOBs.

Time was getting very tight, and the *Sally Queen* was one boat the SOBs didn't want to miss.

The mission was shaping up fast.

Barrabas looked at the forged ID cards Lopez had made. The art of forgery was only half on paper. The other half was the routine that went on in the head of the guy who checked them out. It was a rush job, but Lopez knew his work. They looked perfect. A close examination would blow it, but chances were there wouldn't be a close examination. It was the chance they were taking.

He walked into the next room of the luxurious hotel suite. The equipment they'd spent the morning rounding up was scattered in heaps. The Republic of Panama was strategically centered between the military dictatorships of South America and the guerrilla wars of Central America. The United States government maintained huge installations and large numbers of Army personnel in the Canal Zone. As a result, the country was a discount bargain basement of military hardware and equipment, new and used.

Tiger suits, jungle boots and rucksacks lay on the floor. A table was piled high with morphine syrettes, water purification tablets and insect and leech repellents. Along the floor near the walls were rations, canteens and weapon-cleaning equipment. Pistol belts, harnesses, ammo pouches and knives were neatly laid out in the center of the room. All that was missing were the weapons and the bullets. Lee Hatton and Billy Two were taking care of that.

Nanos, Hayes and O'Toole were sorting equipment and packing the rucksacks. Each merc received an identical pack—right down to the contents of each pocket in the tiger suit. Bayonet on the right harness strap, rappelling snaps on the left. If they had to retrieve something from a dead or wounded team member, no one would waste time looking for it.

Barrabas handed each man his new Panama Canal Company photo ID.

Nanos checked his out. "Hey, Lopez really knows what he's doing when it comes to homemade Xerox. Wait'll you see me sail this baby. I ain't never taken a ship through the Panama Canal before."

"Nanos," Liam O'Toole called across the room, "I'll give you seven to one you don't crash through the locks on the Gatun Spillway and drive the bloody thing right up the middle of the continental divide."

The good-natured put-downs the men traded were a good sign. They were in limbo, their energy building for the job ahead. They let off steam by joking around. Barrabas knew that when they went into action, that same energy was suddenly concentrated and deadly. Each man became a precision fighting instrument. It kept them alive. And winning.

Claude Hayes went on with his work, half listening to Nanos and O'Toole, the rest of his mind somewhere miles away. Barrabas understood Hayes's silence the same way he understood the restlessness of the other men. When Hayes went into action, the silence became hellfire. He'd seen it.

"I've got something, sir!" Beck called from the next room. Barrabas went back and stood over the computer. Beck's hands flew across the keyboard. He was excited.

"She's going through with six other liners at 1400 hours."

"Keep on it, Nate. I want duration and departures from Balboa."

The other three SOBs crowded into the room. Barrabas turned to them.

"Alex, Claude, Liam—you know the details. Once you're on board we'll be with you all the time. Let's move it. We don't have a lot of time. Liam, I'm going to check out progress on the helicopter. Let's rendezvous at 1600 in Panama City."

Barrabas slung his leather jacket over his shoulder and made for the door.

HOT SUN FLOODED DOWN into the street, and the heat pressed against them like lava. Lee Hatton brushed back the hair clinging to her forehead and stepped over the garbage in the road. She scanned the buildings for house numbers. There weren't any.

"Let's try down here." Billy Two led off toward a row of stores, their fronts crossed with iron grilles. Lee followed. Brown children with eyes like saucers ran toward them on bare feet, hands outstretched. They stopped, fished dimes from their pockets and gave them to the children who skipped away, partly in excitement at their newfound wealth, and partly from fear of these strangers who had come to this street.

"It's the same all over, isn't it," said Billy Two.

"The children?"

"Yeah. We could be walking down the streets of Harlem or through some village on an Indian reservation in Arkansas."

They passed the stripped hulk of an old car, and three boys in the metal ruins stopped their playing to stare silently. Panama City had its good neighborhoods and its bad ones. This was the worst.

"There it is—at the end of the next block." With eyes trained by a life of tracking and hunting that had made him the finest survival expert in the U.S. Marine Corps, Billy Two had picked out the rusty sign hung with broken light bulbs from a maze of cables, electric wires and peeling paint on a building a few dozen yards farther on.

"Starlight Lounge. Typical name for this kind of neighborhood."

The rusty back end of an ancient air conditioner dripped water from the slot above a narrow black door. Billy Two pushed it open and they walked in. The bar was dark, but in the half-light they could make out the dirty tile floor and vinyl-covered chairs soiled with the grease of decades. An old man sat at the bar with a drink. He stared at it, lost in thought. His face was red, crisscrossed with channels of tiny veins, and his long silver-white hair was so bright it seemed to glow.

That was the man they were looking for. He was unmistakable, just as the colonel said. Lee Hatton stepped forward.

"Hello." She tried a friendly greeting.

The old man slowly moved away from his drink, turning his head and examining them suspiciously with sharp blue eyes. He said nothing.

"We're looking for Silver John. Know where we can find him?" Lee felt wary under his piercing regard.

There was a long silence as the old man stared at them.

"Maybe," he suddenly cracked. "Depends who wants him. Why. Might be around." His voice was high and thin and as sharp as his eyes. He reached for a can on the counter beside him, pulled out a chaw of greasy tobacco and started chewing. Lee and Billy Two noticed that the silver hair of his beard and mustache were stained yellow. The old man looked at them with defiance.

"We got a message from the colonel—" Billy Two began.

"Silver John don't know no big-shot colonels," the old man interrupted, turning away abruptly. "Don't want no messages from no big-shot colonels." The old-timer went back to his drink and ignored them. Lee tried again.

"Colonel says to tell you the scars don't matter. When the flesh weakens, the will stays strong."

The gnarled hand holding the glass stopped in midair, halfway to the old man's yellow lips. He put the glass down, turned his head, and with a perfectly aimed shot, spat his mouthful of tobacco into a spittoon on the floor by the chair.

"Barrabas!" His voice was a whisper. Silver John was looking at them now. "He remembers what an old man said. Too many years ago."

For a moment the man's eyes clouded with memory, and then suddenly he looked at them again, excited, reaching out his arm to grab Lee by the elbow. "Where is he? He's still alive, is he?" The old man seemed to savor the knowledge.

Lee and Billy Two exchanged glances. The colonel had told them he went back a long way with Silver John, but he hadn't said how long. There was a lot more to their leader than met the eye. It was a thought that occurred to all of the SOBs at one time or another.

"He'll come," Billy Two said. "He needs some things. He sent us ahead."

"He said to tell you he's throwing a party and needs some favors," Lee told the man.

"Throwing a party!" Silver John threw back his head in a laugh that came out as a thin giggle. "Needs some favors. So the boy is still doing business. Yep." He shook his head, a hollow smile folding his cheeks back. "Yep, it's in his blood, that one. Got the magic of a snake charmer, Nile Barrabas has."

The old man jumped off his stool and made his way to the door of the bar. He was filled with sudden life. Lee and Billy Two noticed he walked with a heavy limp, his left leg stiff and unbending at the knee. He slipped the nightbar across the door.

"Come on, come on." The old man waved at them as he stepped crookedly toward the beaded door behind the bar. Lee and Billy Two followed, their curiosity still building. They had a list of weapons and ammunition to pick up from this man. But it wasn't a scenario they had expected.

Silver John led them into a dingy room that was obviously where he lived. Among dozens of empty bottles and piles of yellow newspapers, they could make out a bed.

"Over here." Silver motioned them to stand behind him. He bent over and with astonishing strength shoved the narrow bed aside. Under it, empty chewing tobacco cans littered a soiled mat. The old man threw the mat aside. Lee and Billy Two could barely make out the outline of the trapdoor.

Silver John rummaged through the litter around him until his hand came out with a crowbar. He pried the trapdoor open, heaved it up against the wall and began to descend into darkness on a narrow ladder. As if he suddenly remembered he had company he looked up at Lee and Billy Two. "The party room." He giggled lightly and disappeared into the black hole.

Lee started down after him just as the light came on. At the bottom of the ladder she turned to look at the underground room and let out a low whistle.

"You can say that again," said Billy Two from behind her on the ladder.

The room was lined with concrete, warm and dry. Lee could hear a distant motor running, and she saw vents along the tops of the walls. That would be a dehumidifier. What drew her breath were the guns. M-16s were stacked like firewood, and grenades were packed in crates like tangerines. A Belgian MAG machine gun stood on its tripod and claymores were scattered along the floor. There was enough to equip a small army. Silver John stood in the center of the room gazing at his arsenal, enraptured.

"Where in the name of—" Lee stopped herself. Questions wouldn't be welcome.

Silver John winked. "Left over from a party I threw a few years back."

Billy Two pulled a folded slip of paper from his shirt pocket.

"We brought a list."

The old man picked up an M-16 and stroked the barrel. "I'm not going to be around much longer to take care of all this. If Nile Barrabas wants it, then it'll be well used." He nodded his head thoughtfully. "You just take whatever you want," he said.

IT WAS A DAY LIKE ANY OTHER. Routine.

The security guard sat in his glass booth reading a

magazine. When a car drove up, he opened the door and let in a blast of tropical heat and humidity. The minute it took him to check ID left him drenched with sweat. Then he went back inside and opened the gates to the berthing piers at Cristobal. It took ten minutes for the air conditioning to cool down the glass booth again. It was like that every day. In and out. Hot and cold.

So when the big black Olds pulled up outside his little glass office, the security guard cursed under his breath. He saw the Panama Canal Company license plates. And the three men inside wore expensive business suits. They looked like execs from the head office. He threw down his magazine, hesitated in the coolness another second, then opened the door and plunged into the heat.

The red-haired man in the driver's seat didn't bother to roll down the window. That was routine, too. Executives from the head office didn't get all hot and sweaty like people who worked for a living.

The guard checked out the ID card the driver held up. He had to peer through the tinted glass. He was right. Head office.

The other two men held up similar cards. The guard nodded expressionlessly, walked back to the door of his glass booth and went in. Another blast of hot, humid air followed him. He closed the door, pushed a button, and the gate opened. The Olds drove through. The guard pressed the green button beside the red button. The gate closed. He sat down, muttered another curse and waited for the glass booth to cool off again.

Liam O'Toole stepped on the gas and steered the Olds down the long narrow roadway between the back ends of the berthing piers and the administrative buildings of Cristobal Terminus.

He braked and edged along the wall of a closed warehouse. They had studied the layout of the berthing piers from the plans the colonel had given them. Ahead, at the end of the roadway, lay Limón Bay. Just past the warehouse they could see the stern end of what they'd come for. The *Sally Queen*.

In less than an hour the ship would start its trip through the Panama Canal. It was a tricky procedure, negotiating the five sets of locks to a height of eighty-five feet above sea level, crossing the continental divide, and coming out in the Pacific Ocean. Big ships like the *Sally Queen* didn't go through the delicate locks under their own power. They were hooked to locomotives that pulled them through. As a further precaution, the ship's skipper had to step aside for the duration of the crossing. Skilled navigators, employees of the PCC, went aboard and took over as pilots. And at the same time, a measurer boarded to examine the ship's manifests and papers, to determine the toll fees.

This time, when the *Sally Queen* went through, the pilot would be Alex Nanos, and the measurer Claude Hayes.

"They should be coming any minute," said O'Toole. He had a clear view of the administration building about a half mile down the narrow roadway behind them.

"Luck of the Irish," said Nanos. "There they are."

Two men left the administration building wearing Panama Canal Company jackets. They began the long walk down the road toward the pier where the *Sally Queen* was docked. In the hot, tropical afternoon, the rest of the terminus yards were deserted. Nanos left the car and walked into a deserted loading entrance.

As the Canal Company employees came abreast of the Olds, O'Toole opened the door and got out.

"Charles Jordan?" he asked one of them. A man stepped forward with a questioning look on his face.

"Head Office." O'Toole flipped his ID. "You're the pilot on the *Sally Queen*?"

"That's right. She's due to go through in half an hour."

"And this is the measurer?"

The other man nodded.

O'Toole continued. "We've had a few problems with this ship before. We have evidence the owners have been altering manifests to cheat on toll fees. Let's sit in the car and talk about this. Kind of hot out here."

O'Toole opened the door and motioned. The pilot climbed in the front seat, while the measurer sat in the rear beside Hayes. O'Toole got in and closed the door.

"Well, gentlemen, I'm sorry about all this, I truly am. But sometimes we've got to think of the greater good."

O'Toole and Hayes pulled handguns from under their jackets. With perfect timing, Nanos opened the car door and climbed in, sandwiching the pilot in the front seat.

The Canal Company employees barely registered their surprise before Nanos and Hayes held ether-soaked pads against their mouths and noses. Their struggles ended quickly as they lapsed into unconsciousness.

O'Toole peered carefully up and down the roadway. It was still deserted. "A pity," he remarked. "The poor buggers don't deserve this."

Hayes had a metal case in his lap and was preparing hypodermic syringes. He carefully peered at the tip of the first needle and pressed the plunger until a tiny drop of clear liquid oozed from the point.

"This will put them to sleep until tomorrow. They'll have a little headache and some sore muscles when they wake up, but nothing else."

"And we'll have our asses out of here," said O'Toole.

Hayes injected his needle into the arm of the first man. Within a minute he had finished with both. Nanos and Hayes removed the Panama Canal Company jackets and exchanged them. They took forms and booklets from the briefcases the men had carried and transferred them to their own. The unconscious men were propped up against the seat, and the shoulder harnesses and seat belts were fastened around them.

Nanos and Hayes left the car and began walking toward the *Sally Queen*. The whole operation had taken four minutes.

O'Toole backed the Olds up, turned it around and drove to the gate. When the security guard glanced up from his magazine, he saw three men sitting inside. He pressed the red button and the gates opened. The driver gave him a wave and a big smile and drove through. The guard snorted and went back to reading.

Routine.

BISHOP STOOD BACK, blew out his breath in frustration, and mopped the sweat from his forehead with a greasy hand. It was always the last goddamned nut that wouldn't turn.

He jammed the wrench up against it again. It moved more easily this time. The third adjustment had the nut loose. It was done. The last seat was out. He lifted it and threw it from the helicopter fuselage. Then he stood back to catch his breath.

He still had a hard time believing this was for real.

Twenty-four hours earlier, he told his boss to shove it and kissed his job goodbye. Now he was converting a BK-117 helicopter from a passenger craft recently used by oil exploration engineers to tour the fields of Ecuador into a military craft for a bunch of crazy mercenaries he was just getting to know.

And first impressions when he met them the night before were that some of them were nuts. But tough nuts. Like that last goddamned nut he just took out.

The first thing on order was to chuck the seats. A BK-117 could seat ten. But the SOBs had equipment. And there were other needs for clear space. Like mounting a machine gun in the back door and screwing down the rappel rigging.

It was hard work, and it had been a long time since Bishop had been in the air force. He was glad he kept in shape physically. Then he realized the whole thing was nuts. They were nuts. *He* was nuts. But the whole world was nuts too. He loved it. There was no looking back.

Bishop and Lopez had found the helicopter at the Colón airport, put up for sale by an oil-exploration company facing cutbacks because of the world oil glut. The company was only too glad to sell for cash, and the two SOBs were happy to buy. A BK-117 was a stroke of luck.

The machine was designed in Germany by Messerschmidt-Bolkow-Blohm and was manufactured in Japan by Kawasaki. It was a perfect all-weather craft. Varying humidity conditions affected rotary flight very quickly. The BK-117 could take them from the steamy tropical coastland to the thin air of the mountain cordilleras and even out into the perpetual wind pressure over the waters of the Pacific Ocean.

Two 650-standard-horsepower Avco Lycoming LTS 101 engines gave it a cruising speed of 150 mph, and it could climb at two thousand feet a minute. The advanced Aerospatiale rotor with its glass fiber blades and the flexible hub of forged titanium made it one of the most agile helicopters in the world.

Bishop wiped grease off his hands with a rag and started back to work. Then he felt himself being watched. He turned around.

It was Barrabas.

The colonel stood arms akimbo in the shaft of brilliant

sunlight that pushed through the tall slit between the hangar doors.

His blue eyes looked over the BK-117.

"It's a good helicopter. I've been wondering when they'd get their first military use. Looks like this is it."

"One of the best," Bishop said. "I can do things in this that would be impossible in other helicopters. I can even roll it."

Barrabas strode forward, taking in the long graceful lines of the powerful, wide-bodied craft. He looked at Bishop. The man glowed with sweat, his face streaked with grease. Something about him was different.

"What do you figure on for range?" Barrabas asked.

"Standard is four hundred miles at five thousand feet with maximum payload. And ACL—allowable cargo load—is about four tons, including us. Loaded up, range and maneuverability will be reduced. But most of the time there'll just be Nate and myself. And once we drop the equipment we'll be almost empty."

"And flight fatigue?"

Bishop shook his head.

"Helicopters are hard on pilots because of the vibration. This one has a low vibration level. I can handle it."

"You and Nate are going to have to leapfrog in order to rest, refuel and stay in touch with ground and sea units."

"We can take a reserve. But I've already started plotting every airport, runway and gravel clearing with gas pumps from here to Mexico. Nicaragua might be a problem."

"We'll stay out of Nick. Or try to. The paint job will make it easier." Lopez had used his talents as a forger to paint the oil-company logo back on. The distinctive colors and markings indicated just another company helicopter crowding the airways that led to the riches of

South America. Barrabas had used the ruse as a mercenary many times.

The colonel stuck a cigar in his mouth and held a match to it. As he did so, he flicked his eyes up at Bishop, looking the man over. His intuition about this Canadian pilot was paying off. The man knew what he was doing. Bishop felt the man studying him. He looked back.

Barrabas puffed on the cigar and blew out a funnel of smoke. Then it came to him. Why Bishop looked different. The guy looked as if he'd just had a weight lifted from his shoulders. He looked happy.

Like the other SOBs. At one time or another each of them had been one of the living dead. Jobs, mindless whoring, drinking, prison—there wasn't much difference. A dead end was a dead end.

Mercenary work was different. The challenge of death made every minute a minute to live. Barrabas could see it now in Bishop's face.

The new man would fit in well.

"Let's go for a spin," he told the pilot.

A smile broke like a sunrise across Bishop's face.

"Colonel, she's been waiting for you to say that all day."

Bishop took the helicopter up over Limón Bay. Below them lay the Caribbean coast of Panama. Stretching to the west, it sparkled like an emerald in the afternoon sunlight.

Barrabas had good memories of Panama. Early in his Army career he had been sent to the Jungle Warfare School in the Canal Zone. The Army prepared him for a round of special duties in Vietnam. What he learned about jungles and fighting in them in the Panamanian rain forests provided him with many skills. Skills he used as a paid soldier in the hired armies of a dozen tropical countries on three continents. Skills that had saved his life many times over.

He turned to Bishop and shouted above the noise of the blades.

"Take it out over the bay and turn southeast so we're heading up the canal. Then bring it down at the entrance to the canal so I can get a close look at the ship."

Bishop turned the helicopter over the bay.

The Panama Canal stretched ahead of them like a long razor slash across the green land. Three miles inland the Gatun locks rose in steps up to the watery expanse of Gatun Lake. After negotiating the locks and traversing Gatun Lake, ships arrived at the halfway point marked by the Dariun Locks. There the lift up over the continental divide began, through the narrow rocky Gaillard Cut and down again to Balboa on the Pacific Ocean.

The amazing thing about the Panama Canal was that because of the way Central America twisted sideways on the map, the Atlantic entrance was twenty-seven miles west of the Pacific Ocean. To travel from the Atlantic to the Pacific, ships went from west to east.

One drunken night in a New Jersey bar, on a two-week leave after finishing his jungle warfare training, Barrabas and his buddies from Fort Bragg had bet against the local customers of the Weehawken bar that to travel from the Atlantic to the Pacific, ships had to go east. They walked out five hundred dollars richer.

"That's it." Barrabas nudged Bishop and pointed down.

Directly below them, the berth piers of Cristobal extended out into the bay like teeth from a comb. Ships floated daintily on the flat surface of the water. From this distance, it was like looking over the edge of a bathtub filled with a kid's model toys. Bishop brought the copter down until they were only a few hundred feet over the surface of the bay.

At the entrance to the canal, a line of eight ships was

preparing to enter. The *Sally Queen* was easy to spot. A rusting two-decked steamer, she flew the Liberian flag and stood out among the glistening paint jobs of the bulk carriers and container ships in front of and behind her.

Barrabas heard a steady beep from the radio beside him and switched it on. Beck's voice wavered through the scrambler.

"O'Toole reports all successful, but I have bad news. I ran through the next twenty-four hours on the PCC computer. It looks like they've got a scheduled stop for unloading at the other end in Balboa. They're due out of Balboa at midnight."

"Can you get a destination for the goods?" Barrabas asked.

"I doubt it. That kind of info isn't in the PCC computer, but I can give it a try."

"All right, Nate, we're coming down soon. Hold tight." Barrabas clicked off the receiver.

The *Sally Queen* was now about an eighth of a mile to his left, sitting heavily in the water, her masts and booms supporting an oily spiderweb of winches and lines. Barrabas looked along the decks and the two bridges. There was no sign of activity. The sailors would be relaxing somewhere below, making use of this time to do nothing.

Suddenly he could feel anger building in his gut.

In the iron belly of the rusting ship, a deadly cargo of G-11s and LANCE missiles waited. Those weapons had a destiny. Someone wanted to destroy American efforts to bring peace to war-torn Central America.

He'd already murdered five American soldiers in cold blood to do it.

He was going to use those weapons to kill more.

The politicians in Washington had called in the SOBs. It was out of their hands now.

Barrabas would take care of it. But not for some two-faced government policy that never knew which way it was looking.

He'd do it for those five murdered men.

And he'd do it his own way.

Soldiers didn't have a lot of rights in this world. But they had the right to die in battle. Not slaughtered like animals, the way those advisors in El Salvador had been killed, and the soldiers in Kaiserslauten. Or the way a man named Karl Heiss had butchered his men in Vietnam years before.

People forget.

Politicians forget.

Nile Barrabas didn't.

He was going to find who was responsible. And he was going to destroy him. Or die trying.

5

The captain of the *Sally Queen* greeted the two men from the Panama Canal Company when they arrived on the lower level of the two-story bridge. They climbed the stairs to the navigation room. A tall blond man waited there.

"Let me introduce you to Mr. Beam," said the captain. "He's a representative of the company whose cargo we're carrying."

"How d'ya do?" the man said in an easy California accent. "Purchasing agent for Nastex Agricultural Importers."

Beam's eyes flicked back and forth between the two men. Claude Hayes saw something in those eyes he didn't like. Recognition.

Nanos began to examine the instrument panels.

Hayes drew a clipboard from his briefcase.

"I'll need manifests and ship's papers," he said. "And I'll want to inspect the holds."

A look of alarm crossed Beam's face. He exchanged looks with the captain.

"Isn't that a bit unusual?" the captain said.

"New policy," Hayes explained. "We've had some evidence that certain companies have been altering their manifests to lower the toll rates." Hayes gave them a friendly smile. "I'm sure there won't be any problems. Just a cursory look."

The blond American's face darkened. "This is outrageous! These papers are enough. I want to speak to your boss about this.''

"Certainly, sir," Nanos replied. "You can phone him now. Of course it will mean a delay in going through the canal, and the next transit is, let me see—" he glanced at his watch "—six hours from now."

"It's just a random check," said Hayes. "To·compare document numbers on some of the crates below to what you've got written here.''

The captain and Beam looked at each other again. Beam was still angry.

"All right. We'll get a seaman to show you the holds. I don't know why you're bothering, though.''

While the others were occupied, Nanos slipped a transmitter disk onto the underside of the radio panel.

A few minutes later a sailor arrived at the bridge to accompany Hayes.

The old ship creaked, and Hayes felt it beginning to move. The eight-hour journey through the canal had begun. As he moved forward into the ship, he carefully memorized its layout.

SILVER JOHN GLANCED down Billy Two's list, his eyes lighting up as he ticked off the items.

"M-16 or equivalents, grenades of the antipersonnel and antitank variety, and incendiaries. Sniper rifles. Got some good British L4A1s somewhere here. M-60 I don't have, but that MAG is a damned good machine gun. Image-intensification night devices, flash suppressors and silencers for automatic rifles. Looks as if Nile's fighting a stealth war.''

He looked at Billy Two and Lee questioningly. Then he put his hand up.

"That's all right—you don't have to tell me nothing. I got something here I think you'll find useful, though.

Made by the Belgians. Clever, those Belgians are. I know. I worked with them. In the Congo. Few years back. It's called Jet Shot—a grenade launcher—and it's silent, flashless and smokeless.''

Silver John rummaged in a corner of the room and turned around holding up handfuls of PRB antipersonnel grenades. ''It's just a special cartridge fitted into the tail boom of these here grenades. Needs a special launcher. I got some.'' Again the old man started poking around the boxes of weapons.

''The colonel will be here in a while. Why don't we get started and see what he says?'' Lee suggested.

It took Lee and Billy Two less than an hour to choose what they needed from Silver John's collection and stack it in the middle of the room. The old guy watched them, his eyes greedy with pleasure as he entertained them with stories about the firing power of each weapon as it came off the wall. And Silver John knew his rifles.

He was ecstatic when Billy Two came across a couple of rare Czechoslovakian Skorpion machine pistols.

''A real machine pistol,'' he said, turning the ten-inch-long gun over in his hand. ''Not many of these around. The size of a Mauser and seven hundred rounds a minute. What the 7.65mm bullets lack in stopping power is made up in speed. You want a few of these?''

Billy Two looked at it, mulling it over. A machine pistol had limited use. That was why there weren't many of them around. But it was compact, easily concealed, and it would be useful in tight situations and confined spaces. Like on board a ship.

''Sure,'' said Billy Two. ''Nanos and Lopez will love it for the job they've got coming up.''

He stacked a couple of the Skorpions beside the short, close-quarter Colt Commando versions of the Armalite he had put aside.

They went upstairs, closed up the trapdoor and

waited. The colonel arrived in less than an hour with Lopez behind him.

For a brief moment Silver John was speechless when Barrabas walked in the door. Tears filled his eyes. The old man and the soldier embraced like long-lost friends. Silver John stood back to take a good look at Barrabas.

"Well, I'll be! If you aren't turning into Nile Silver. Just like me!" He grabbed a handful of his own long silver hair and held it up, cackling at the comparison.

Barrabas gave an embarrassed smile. "I took a bullet at Kap Long. It healed, but it left me with the hair as a reminder."

"The scars don't matter!" The old man raised his finger with a twinkle in his eye.

"The will is strong," Barrabas finished for him and slapped him on the back. "How's the leg?"

"Gets me around, gets me around. You hadn't got me out of there, there wouldn't be any leg. Wouldn't be any Silver John, either."

"That war was a long time ago." Barrabas's thoughts drifted for a moment to a jungle years before. "You were a good commander."

"You were a good soldier. You ever going to collect that medal you got waiting for you somewhere in Washington?"

Barrabas shrugged. He slipped a thick brown envelope out of his jacket.

"What's the bill, Silver John?"

"Oh, I think that'll about do it," the old man answered, eyeing the envelope. Barrabas gave it to him with a smile.

"I'm always glad to throw business a friend's way."

Silver John winked again and motioned to Lee and Billy Two standing by the bar trying not to listen.

"You got some soldiers these days, Nile. Gotta say,

the world's a'changin'. Could'a used a few like that in my time. Lighten the load, eh?''

"She's good." Barrabas looked over to Lee, who was smiling in amusement.

"Oh, I know she is," Silver John said with conviction. "Didn't I see her down there handling those M-16s? That's one girl knows her guns. But what are we standing here gabbing for? You got a war to fight, Nile, and I don't want to know nothing about it, but you just get that stuff you want out of here. Soldier, what you got out there, whatever it is, drive it around back.''

Lopez's white teeth flashed under his mustache as he turned to look out the door. "Man, I found us a paddy wagon that belonged to a used dictator. Under the paint job there's armor plating. It gets three miles to the gallon, but stops bullets." Lopez's talent for scavenging pulled through again.

NIGHT CAME QUICKLY. There was little twilight that far south. O'Toole and Lopez sat at the wheel of a Buick parked outside the entrance to the Balboa Terminus. The black Olds had been abandoned in some trees off the highway out of Cristobal on the other side of the country. The next morning the two Panama Canal Company employees would wake up, stiff from sitting up in the car all night. They'd wonder where the hell they were. But they'd be all right.

The *Sally Queen* had just pulled into the Balboa pier. They saw Nanos and Hayes emerge from the entrance to the Terminus yards and pulled the Buick around to let them in.

Nanos whooped with excitement as he got in the car.

"Hey, another notch in my belt! One ship through the Panama Canal! Find me an orange crate and I'll sail it to Tierra del Fuego!''

O'Toole turned the car around and veered off down the highway that ran along the Bay of Panama.

"Wet suits?" Hayes's voice was businesslike. They weren't finished yet.

"In the trunk." O'Toole turned back to look at the men. "You saw them unloading?"

Hayes spoke. "Yeah. The big crates from the forward hold. It has to be the missiles. Too big for rifles or ammo. It's all set up. There's a garbage door off the galley on the port side open for us and rope hanging down. The holds are open, too."

"Let's get our asses moving so you can get aboard while they're unloading."

O'Toole pulled the car off the road into the bushes that bordered the highway. In less than a minute, Lopez and the men who had just left the *Sally Queen* as employees of the Panama Canal Company were putting on wet suits to go back in a more official capacity. As the Soldiers of Barrabas.

"Just us and the rats hiding out down there in the holds," Lopez joked as he zipped the black rubber around him.

"Rats?" Nanos's voice was filled with mock fear. "No one told me anything about rats."

"They're great company. Back on the Lower East Side in New York they were always the life of the party. Used to open the beer with their teeth. Sharp little teeth." Lopez smiled wickedly. "They just love sinking them into hot Greeks."

"If the women who love me knew the company I keep," Nanos lamented, shaking his head sadly.

The men fastened their wet suits deftly and donned masks and snorkels. O'Toole handed each of them a long, waterproof case that they attached to their backs.

"Baby, I love you," said Lopez, kissing the case before strapping it on. "Life on that ship could get dangerous without an automatic rifle. Lots of places to hide, but nowhere to run.''

"If worst comes to worst, I can use it on the rats," said Nanos.

Hayes finished last, tightening the straps on the case of the portable radio unit around his waist. When they were ready they stood silently by the edge of the water.

O'Toole looked at them. "We'll be with you all the time. If you pick up any interesting conversations from the bridge, let us know. And if there's trouble, Bishop can have the helicopter there in five minutes. Good luck."

Nanos, Hayes and Lopez slipped silently into the Pacific waters like shadows cut from the fabric of night.

BARRABAS PEERED THROUGH BINOCULARS at the Balboa loading docks. It was midnight. The blue-white arc lights that lit up the bustling activity along the pier gave the landscape a sinister eeriness. Almost before the ship had stopped, booms were swinging, wires and winches craned and hold doors were opened back. Very quickly, large wooden crates swung across the side of the ship onto a loader and disappeared into a warehouse.

An hour earlier, a truck had driven inside the yards.

The SOBs parked the van a quarter of a mile up the road from the Balboa Terminus and waited.

In the back, Lee Hatton and Billy Two pored over maps of Central America, marking landing zones, routes, rally points and evacuation routes up the length of the Pacific coast.

"Looks good, Colonel," said Lee. "We'll be driving five miles inland. The *Sally Queen* will probably stay in international waters twelve miles offshore. With Bishop and Nate in between in the helicopter, we'll keep our communications."

Barrabas put down the binoculars. The helicopter was

a communications central between his landborne and seaborne contingents. It was an axiom of war that no plan survived contact with the enemy. Contact was imminent. Communication among the separate attack units was vital. If they lost contact, they'd be in deep trouble.

"*If* the truck goes north," Barrabas said. "That's the gamble we're taking." It was the logical choice. From Panama there were only two directions to go. South America wasn't in the picture as far as he could figure. That meant Costa Rica. Or Nicaragua. The ship was headed for Mexico. But logic didn't always work out in this kind of game. If the trucks didn't go north, the SOBs would be split in two.

Barrabas heard a van door opening and turned to see Liam O'Toole climbing into the driver's seat.

"How'd it go?"

"Good. If they're on, we'll be hearing any minute."

"Are the men working well together?"

"When Nanos and Lopez stop ribbing each other, they are."

"That's all right. If they can take each other's jokes, they respect each other. It means they'll fight well together, too."

The radio on the seat beside Barrabas bleeped. It was Beck.

"They're on board, Colonel."

The distant sound of metal doors sliding open and shifting gears made Barrabas look up. A truck was pulling out of the loading gate and turning onto the highway.

Over the tops of the warehouse roof he could see the masts of the *Sally Queen* sliding forward as the ship moved out to sea.

"Roger, Nate. The truck is out. Give us visuals from their running lights."

The truck turned left toward the coast highway. It was going north. The gamble had paid off.

O'Toole turned on the ignition as the red taillights disappeared down the highway. He slipped the van into gear and pulled out onto the road.

A sliver of moon glimmered over the rolling waters of the Bay of Panama. The narrow, grassy Pacific coast lay shrouded in darkness. Soon the road turned inland toward the low mountains, the Sierra de Veragua.

Barrabas lay back in his seat as the highway flew by, feeling the steady vibrations of the engine. He rolled down the window and breathed in the Pacific air. Everything had gone well so far.

But he knew as sure as the first light of dawn appeared in the east that the new day wouldn't end without a fight.

6

Bishop banked the helicopter thirty degrees to take the western sun from his eyes. The cones of volcanoes straddling the top of the Cordillera de Guanacaste were carpeted bright green. The sky was still blue even though there was only a half hour of daylight left. There was no twilight in the tropics. In half an hour it would be dark.

"It's at ten o'clock." Nate Beck was in the seat beside him, peering through the glass bubble with binoculars. Bishop could just make out the dinky toy truck pulling along a narrow dirt road up the side of a volcano.

It took all day for the truck to cross Panama and climb north into Costa Rica. When Bishop brought the helicopter down for rest and refueling in San José, O'Toole kept after them in the van. It looked as if the truck were heading for Nicaragua. Just before the border it pulled off onto a road leading through Costa Rican coffee plantations in a valley below the two-thousand-foot-high Ortosi volcano.

"There's a ranch or something up there," said Beck, still on the binoculars. Bishop kept the helicopter straight on course while Beck radioed the van. Barrabas's voice quavered back through the scrambler. The colonel wanted reconnaissance.

The truck was climbing the western slope. At a maximum speed of 170 miles per hour, the BK-117 spun around the cone of the volcano like a stone in a sling.

Beck hung on, his momentary terror giving way to a joke.

"It's better than Crack-the-Whip at the midway."

"Sorry," Bishop apologized. "Been a few years since I flew one of these. I get a little carried away. After ten years of flying those sluggish passenger jets, getting back into a helicopter is like going from a tourist bus to a motorcycle."

The flat blue surface of Lake Nicaragua flashed just across the border to one side as Bishop brought the helicopter around the mountain. The sun was in his eyes again. And setting fast. They didn't have much time.

Beck peered across at the volcano. The truck was pulling into a walled compound on a thin plateau halfway up the side. A whitewashed villa with the red tile roof typical of Costa Rica dominated the space inside the walls. Behind it and farther back up the mountain slope stood a windowless building with a shed roof that faced north toward Lake Nicaragua. The dying sun glittered on strips of metal running down the surface of the roof. The top was a door. The building was a silo.

"There's our missile." Beck pointed at the building.

Bishop kept the helicopter on a straight line across the volcano toward La Cruz, six miles away. A group of men had come from the buildings and gathered around the truck.

"Let's get word to the colonel," said Bishop. "Looks like we'll be back tonight."

GLEN BEAM FELT BETTER with every mile that went by as the truck crossed Panama and Costa Rica. Every foot up the side of the volcano brought him closer to the completion of his project. Arms smuggling had never appealed to him. He did it because the price was right.

The first shipment had been easy. Straight to Honduras. This time there were rifles on the ship and the missile for Costa Rica. It was complicated. In a few hours he would fly to the ship to supervise the transfer of the rifles. Then Jeremiah would pay him. Then Beam would disappear.

Forever. With a new identity. Jeremiah, Beam had decided, was a dangerous man.

The truck slowed and drove in through the open gates of the compound. Beam climbed out of the cab, stretched his legs and looked around. It was beautiful here. Lovely. The white Spanish-style hacienda was surrounded by a long low veranda to shade the interior from the hot sun. Around it spread gardens. And in front, water tinkled from three spouts into the basin of a fountain.

A short thin Latin American walked across the sun-baked ground in tight jeans and shiny snakeskin cowboy boots. It was Diego. He had a friendly smile. Smiles come easy when they have an SMG to back them up. Diego carried an Uzi, his prize possession. The former National Guard officer had brought it with him when he fled Nicaragua after the Sandinista takeover.

"Señor Glen, you have been successful. I congratulate you. Come. We will drink to your success in the house."

"Let's get that thing to the silo while we have some light, Diego. Then we will drink to success."

Beam saw sunlight glint off a helicopter flying along the edge of the volcano almost a mile away. The helicopter came closer, then passed toward the coast. It belonged to an oil company.

The Latin American smiled again. "Certainly, Señor Glen. When we are finished."

A half-dozen men already surrounded the truck with wrenches and drills to slip off the false fuel tank and take out the missile. Diego snapped at the men in rapid Spanish. They hurried faster.

"You have a helicopter for me?" Beam asked.

"Yes. Behind the house. And you will tell Jeremiah we have done everything. That we await only his word."

"Yes. I'll tell Jeremiah everything. I'll tell him what a good job you and your men have done here."

"Ah, Señor Glen—to be back in Managua again! I have waited a long time to destroy the Sandinistas."

"And to get back to your helicopter stunts."

"Señor!" Diego looked offended. "My reputation is unfair! To throw children from helicopters...." He shrugged. "It was only to show our power. Regrettable but necessary."

"We all do only what's necessary." The Nicaraguan government was searching high and wide for Diego because of certain indiscreet atrocities he committed during the civil war. Beam couldn't have cared less.

Diego's men slipped the missile from the belly of the truck and loaded its thirteen hundred pounds onto a forklift vehicle. They drove it up the incline of the plateau toward the silo. Beam and the ex-National Guard officer followed.

"Jeremiah is a great man," Diego said admiringly. "I have waited a long time for my revenge. He has given me the weapons."

"Yes," said Beam. "A great man."

And completely insane, Beam had decided. The road to Jeremiah had been a strange one. At the beginning, and now, at the very end.

The beginning was in 1968 in the Haight-Ashbury. Glen Beam had left Hicksville, U.S.A., for San Francisco as had thousands of other kids who wanted in on free love and flower power. Unlike most of them, however, he knew an opportunity when he saw one.

The opportunity was drugs. Speed, heroin, STP, acid. It stopped being profitable when his customers kept dying.

Then he met Jeremiah. The man preached sermons in Golden Gate Park. People were attracted to him because he talked about love and peace and building a new society. The fact that he was a giant seemed to add to his powerful charisma. Maybe it was fear. People found him persuasive. So did the government. Jeremiah skimmed off lots in grants.

One day Jeremiah approached Beam with a special order. Sedatives, Pentothal compounds, potassium cyanides. And the price was very, very good.

Soon Jeremiah had his own community center and hundreds of converts. Then thousands. His followers did everything for him. Only Beam knew the secret of Jeremiah's success. Chemical mind control.

Even Diego's slavish respect for his benefactor had its origins in Beam's drugs. Beam knew that. Diego and his men didn't. Beam was getting out. Before Jeremiah got to him, too.

Diego and Beam entered the shedlike silo building.

The missile was being winched high into the rafters and lowered onto its launching cradle. The control panel was beside it. It was easy to operate. There was only a button. It was just a matter of setting the coordinates.

Beam picked up a hand grenade from an opened crate lying on the floor and began tossing it back and forth in his hands.

"Diego, when you get the word from Jeremiah, press this." Beam pointed to a series of buttons beside a key lock on the control panel. "Simple. Instant blast-off. Instant death. Eight hundred little bombs all over the place. Bye-bye Managua. Bye-bye Sandinistas." He continued to juggle the grenade back and forth in his hands.

Diego's eyes lit up. "Ah, Señor Glen. Never in my life have I felt happier. Now we must drink to our success."

They left the silo and walked toward the house. Beam kept the grenade.

AT ABSOLUTE LAST LIGHT, Barrabas saw a helicopter fly out of the mountainside compound. Then darkness came as if a blanket had suddenly been thrown over the sun. The heat was gone. In the high cordillera the temperature plunged at night. The five-mile trek ahead of them would warm them up.

He stared down at the map Billy Two was holding out for him. It showed northern Costa Rica and the border area along Nicaragua. The markings on it were the latest intelligence information on *contra* camps, poised to attack Nicaragua from their Costa Rican bases. Most of them were in the eastern part of the country near Misquito Indian territory. A few were hidden in border-area volcanic valleys where the rivers flowing into Lake Nicaragua made transportation easy. The compound on the side of the Ortosi crater wasn't marked. Whoever was up there, American intelligence didn't know about them.

O'Toole gave the inside of the van a last look. It was another five miles uphill on the gravel road to the ranch. They'd do that on foot. He drove the van into the forest. Some lucky farmer would find it in a few days if the SOBs didn't come back for it.

"I want prisoners." Barrabas bit the end off his cigar and spat it out. He lit it.

Billy Two tightened his ammunition belt while Lee strapped a ring of grenades around her waist. Barrabas shouldered a single-spigot Jet Shot grenade launcher, while O'Toole heaved the heavy multispigot launcher onto his back. Silver John's weaponry was going to get its first test.

"When we kill, we kill as silently as possible. Use your flash suppressors. And no fires. If any of those buildings go up, they'll be visible for miles up and down this valley." Barrabas folded the map and handed it back to Billy Two.

They quick-marched four miles up the dark road. Deep in the forest of oak and mountain pine, the night eyes of possums shone like silver coins. The last mile was through the forest. An hour later they were at the ranch. There was a hundred-foot clearing between the edge of the forest and the stone walls.

The high wooden gate was closed. The compound inside was bathed in the soft glow of lights set on poles throughout the grounds. There was no visible sign of security. No guards. No defensive precautions. It looked easy. Too easy.

"Wait here," Barrabas whispered. He moved back into the forest and silently circled the compound. He stopped frequently to peer along the ground at the edge of the clearing. Then he saw it.

It was only about a foot and a half high, and in the darkness its shape almost melted into the shrubs and undergrowth of the forest. It took a careful eye to spot the tripod and the horizontal barrel of the microwave fence system.

Barrabas crept up to the barrel. Its long end faced down the edge of the clearing. Two hundred feet away there was another one. Between them was an invisible curtain of energy. The pods would encircle the camp. Each was connected by a cable to a control unit or remote alarm. If anyone cut the cable, the alarm would go off. Barrabas moved back to the SOBs.

"They have the place surrounded by a microwave intruder system set up at the edge of the clearing. Stay in the forest."

He looked at his watch. It was 2345. "O'Toole, Hatton—we'll go for midnight. When you hear the action starting, it won't matter about the intruder system anymore. Billy Two, let's go."

Barrabas and Billy Two circled around the compound through the tangled pine forest, working their way up the slope of the volcano. Billy Two dropped into position overlooking the ranchhouse. Barrabas went higher up the slope until he could see the entire compound stretched out below.

The truck had been parked at the back of the house, beside the frame building with the shed roof. Wide garage doors spilled light into the yard. A half-dozen men holding FN FAL rifles and Uzi submachine guns stood around the truck.

Barrabas set up the Jet Shot launcher on its tripod and adjusted the azimuth. Then he pulled the PRB grenade from his belt and attached it by the special Jet Shot cartridge to the launcher.

The second hand on his watch swept around toward midnight. He aimed for the crowd of men standing around the truck and pressed the firing switch.

Silver John was dead on. Silent. Without flash or smoke.

Two of them saw it just as it arrived over their heads. Then it blew. They were thrown back like rag dolls.

A couple of men picked themselves up from the ground, their faces bloody. They turned for the house. They weren't a problem.

But the men with submachine guns suddenly pouring out of the ranchhouse were.

Billy Two's flash-suppressed M-16 spilled autofire back and forth in front of their feet.

Barrabas had a second grenade on its way.

The men in the compound fired back wildly at their unseen and unheard adversaries. The survivors from the concussion attack were caught in the cross fire. They twitched and jerked, then dropped to the ground. The second grenade blew, and the survivors ran for the house.

Blind return fire poured from inside, climbing up the slope toward Barrabas's position. They still hadn't located their attackers, but they were getting close. Billy Two sent it back inside the windows of the villa.

Barrabas zigzagged down the slope toward the silo.

"BLOODY HELL, it's good to get that off my back," O'Toole grunted, heaving the grenade launcher over his shoulder as he and Lee took up their position opposite the front gates.

The multispigot launcher would launch twelve grenades in series of two. The last two fired before the first two hit the ground. It gave the illusion of a mass attack even though it was operated by one person on a remote. It was also a Jet Shot device; by the time the enemy had figured out they'd been hit, they were dead. But it was also heavy to carry. O'Toole was exhausted. He'd just carried it five miles uphill. His face ran with sweat.

"Take a break, soldier. I'll set it up." Lee went to work attaching the cartridges into the tail booms of the PRB grenades and shoving them onto the spigots. She adjusted the azimuth. Then she attached a Mecar 40mm antitank grenade to O'Toole's M-16.

It was almost midnight. Lee Hatton was ready. She checked her watch again and handed O'Toole his rifle.

"In thirty seconds we'll see if this system works."

O'Toole sighted down the graduated grid on his rifle. "Knock, knock, who's there?" he said in a low voice.

A few seconds later, from the mountainside behind the house, grenades talked back, followed by the rapid answer of autofire.

Barrabas, that's who.

Lee flicked the electronic release. It took a millisecond for the charge to blow. It worked like a charm.

In almost total silence, the grenades left their spigots and sailed gracefully through the air like clay pigeons. Silver John was right. The first grenades blew inside the compound just as the last two took off.

O'Toole pulled the trigger on his M-16.

The 5.56mm round blew the grenade straight into the gates, sending them up in a cloud of smoke and debris. The cloud rained splinters of wood. The gate was a gaping hole.

The last of the PRB grenades anti'd any remaining personnel inside the front compound.

Lee sent a burst of rifle fire through the opening for good measure, covering O'Toole as he ran for the side of the gate. There was no reply.

The Irishman flattened himself up against the wall and pulled the pin on a PRB offensive hand grenade and tossed it up over the wall.

Lee made a run for the opposite side of the open gate. The blast of the offensive grenade kept her covered until she made it.

They could hear the windows of the house shattering under the assault from Billy Two's autofire.

O'Toole gave Lee a nod.

A fast ninety-degree pivot faced them into the front yard. They decorated the stucco house with bullet holes. If anyone had been alive in the front yard, they were dead now. Everyone else was still busy out back.

There was no resistance.

BARRABAS HIT THE SIDE OF THE SILO shed when the gates blew out front. A man with an Uzi fired at him from the back door of the villa. Bullets tore at the wood over his head.

Billy Two sent out a withering line of bullets. The man sprayed pink up against the white stucco house. His Uzi flew into the air. He landed snakeskin cowboy boot toes up.

Billy Two went back to knocking out windows.

They'd driven the enemy into the cage Barrabas wanted them in. The SOBs kept them busy, crouching low and eating floorboards as waves of autofire whipped the house.

With single shots, Barrabas took out a couple of lights that the grenades hadn't hit. The compound was almost dark now except for light streaming from the silo.

He crept slowly around the corner of the building, concussion grenade in hand. When he came up beside the open door, he bit out the pin, counted to five and spun it low inside. He covered his ears. The wooden wall behind him bulged from the impact of the explosion.

He turned low inside the door, his Armalite up, finger itching on the trigger. He didn't need to fire.

The missile launcher was poised in the center of the room, and the missile was strapped in like a papoose on its mother's back. A man rolled in pain along the dirt floor, trying to pick himself up. Blood streamed from his ears and nose. Then he saw Barrabas.

He grabbed for the gun lying on the floor beside him. Barrabas shot first. The gun flew from the man's hand, and most of the hand went with it. He screamed. His armed sprayed blood from severed wrist arteries like an out-of-control firehose.

Barrabas went down on his knees and grabbed the mangled arm. He didn't want the guy dying. Not yet. He had a few questions to ask. Then the guy could do what he liked.

He dug his fingers deep into the arteries under the man's bicep muscles to stop the flow.

It didn't make any difference.

Air grated into the man's lungs with a horrible rasping sound. His chest heaved up as his back arched. Two great white eyes popped out of the bloody face like— like eggs, thought Barrabas. Like the cyanide eggs they use in gas chambers.

The body stiffened and quivered. The chest collapsed. The bubble eyes stared upward, round and dead.

Barrabas dropped the arm. The bleeding had stopped. So had the heart.

Then he noticed it. The rifle fire outside had stopped, too.

He left the silo and ran for Billy Two who crouched behind the parked truck. Barrabas squatted beside him.

"It just stopped—all of a sudden! Tried to wake them up with a few rounds, but no response."

Barrabas pulled his RT-10 from his belt.

"Hatton, O'Toole—what's happening?"

Lee's voice came through from the other side of the compound. "Colonel, we got dead silence and no reaction."

"Lob some grenades up against the house," Barrabas ordered. "Then hold fire and wait for instructions."

The explosions blew great chunks of masonry off the house and sent red clay tiles dancing off the roof. Still silence.

Barrabas cupped his hands and yelled in Spanish, "The next ones go inside! You have thirty seconds to appear at the door without your weapons and surrender. After thirty seconds we blow the house."

Thirty seconds passed very slowly for the mercs. Very fast for whoever was inside.

No one appeared at the door of the villa.

Lee and Billy Two covered the windows with autofire again. Barrabas and O'Toole ran across the open ground on each side of the house.

Barrabas stood with his back pressed tight against the wall of the house. He lit a flare and tossed it through the open window. Then he ran across the window, firing down into the room. He had just enough time to see that it was empty.

O'Toole was doing the same thing on the other side.

Barrabas's radio crackled. It was O'Toole.

"Colonel, our problems are over. There's no one alive in there. But you've gotta see it for yourself."

Slowly Billy Two and Barrabas entered the dark villa. Bits of light from sputtering flares did a wild shadow dance in the hallway. The bullets had done their work. The interior was in shambles. Glass, plaster and splinters of wood snapped under their boots. O'Toole and Lee came in the other way.

"In there." O'Toole pointed with his rifle.

It was a radio room. The front of the big set was chewed up by 5.56 rounds. The bodies were in a big pile four feet high.

There were twelve of them, stiff, their heads pulled back, eyes staring, lips drawn, teeth clenched in smiles of death.

"Cyanide," said Lee. She leaned over a body and pulled back the mouth. "Tooth capsule."

"And no prisoners," said Barrabas. "They were ready for us after all."

BARRABAS LOOKED OVER BECK'S SHOULDER as the electronics wizard went over the missile-control panel.

"This baby's set for Nicaragua," Beck announced. "Downtown Managua. And with an accuracy range of about thirty yards, it would have been deadly. Someone's not too hot on Sandinistas. Besides Uncle Sam."

"Can you rig it to blow up here?" Barrabas asked.

"It can be done. Might blow away half the mountainside, but it can be done." Beck pulled a small toolbox from his rucksack. He held up an alarm clock. "Primitive but effective. When should I set it for?"

"Set it up, and we'll wait until we hear from Hayes and the others on the ship. I'll take the radio tonight. You and the others sleep."

They'd been up thirty-six hours now. Four of them had just fought a battle, and Bishop and Beck had been up in a helicopter all day. They were exhausted. And they'd just gotten started. It was the first thing a commander made sure of. That his soldiers were rested.

He walked out into the compound. O'Toole and Bishop were going over the BK-117. Around front, Lee and Billy Two stood outside the house. Barrabas walked toward them.

"Colonel, we found these inside the radio room." Lee held up some notebooks she and Billy were looking at. Sweat had streaked the black camouflage paint on her face. Her M-16 was slung over her shoulder. For a moment Barrabas realized her beauty was devastating.

"Radio codes," said Billy Two.

"We'll give them to Nate to check out. You two find a place out by the helicopter and get some sleep."

They nodded.

Barrabas surveyed the yard. Halfway to the blasted remains of the front gate, water tinkled softly into the basin of an ornamental fountain, oblivious to the surrounding carnage.

He felt a cold chill. It wasn't the night temperature.

"I feel it too, Colonel." It was Lee, standing at his shoulder. He could feel her breath against his neck.

"I've known soldiers who'd killed themselves rather than surrender because they knew their fate as prisoners would be worse than dying," said Barrabas. "But somehow this doesn't fit in."

"Whatever it is," said Billy Two, "it's going to get crazier."

Barrabas nodded silently.

7

Claude Hayes stretched his long body and rotated his head to flex the muscles of his neck and shoulders.

"The engines have stopped." Nanos's voice came out of the darkness. Beside him, Lopez sat with the receiver, his face illuminated by dial glow. With the transistorized earphones wrapped around his head, he listened in rapt concentration for conversations from the bridge.

The ship still creaked as it slid through the water, but the rhythmic pounding of the giant engines, which had reverberated through the hold for the last twenty-four hours, was gone. The three men had sat quietly and in darkness for a long time. They took turns monitoring conversations from the bridge. Now the engines had stopped. There was silence in the dark, smelly hold. The silence that comes before a storm.

Nanos stood and stretched. They'd been cooped up in that hold far too long. He wanted to beat his chest and scream like Tarzan. He wanted to start running, to breathe fresh air again. He wanted a fight. He had the feeling he'd get what he wanted in short order.

"I want Beam," said Hayes, gripping the wooden butt of the Skorpion machine pistol. They'd picked up Beam's voice in the bridge hours ago. He was back on the ship. The man's face had frozen itself in Hayes's memory.

"I've seen eyes like that before. I've seen eyes like that beating black brothers in Alabama. I've seen eyes like that whipping prisoners in that Georgia chain gang where I did my time. You know what those eyes say to me, Greek?''

Nanos didn't answer.

Hayes looked back, his eyes impassive, strong, deadly.

"Nothing. They're empty. Empty eyes. He's got no soul in there. Just something dead. He is one evil mother.''

Hayes aimed his Skorpion straight ahead of him and extended his arm as if about to shoot. *"Pow!* Right in the middle of the forehead. Something for Beam to think about. A lead lobotomy.'' He looked back at Nanos. "Leave Beam to me.''

"They're receiving something on the bridge.'' Lopez's voice was urgent. "Hayes, take a copy.''

Hayes snapped on a wristlight and jotted down figures as Lopez dictated what he heard from the bridge.

"Positon 86 degrees 35 minutes by 12 degrees 70 minutes.'' Lopez stopped and listened, his brow tight in concentration.

Nanos spread a small plasticized map out under Hayes's light and charted with his finger across the meridian and latitude.

"That puts us fifty miles off the Nicaraguan coast just north of Costa Rica.''

"They're setting up a ship-to-ship rendezvous,'' said Lopez, listening intently.

"From Nicaragua?'' Nanos asked.

Lopez shook his head. "I dunno. The ship arrives here in five hours. It's in the water a hundred miles northwest of here. That's it. They're waiting now.'' He pulled the earphones off and looked up at Nanos and Hayes.

"We wait or we go?'' asked Nanos.

"We go.'' Hayes picked his Commando up and slung

it over his shoulder. "Through the engine room. We clean the ship out from the bottom up." Hayes pulled his knife from its sheath and stuck it between his teeth as he adjusted his cartridge belt. Nanos stared at him.

"What are you staring at, Greek?" Hayes demanded between clenched teeth.

It was a vision of hellfury.

"I was just thinking," said Nanos, "that I'd hate to be on the enemy side of a guy like you."

The three mercs moved forward to a thick steel door that separated the hold from the engine room. They slipped into a gallery overlooking the pit. Two men leaned over the big engines, making adjustments to the machinery. Their backs were to them.

"Like shooting rats in a barrel," Nanos whispered. He motioned for Hayes and Lopez to stay, then quietly descended the narrow metal stairs into the pit.

The problem with shooting rats in a barrel was the ricochet off the metal walls. This had to be done more carefully. Besides, they wanted prisoners.

Nanos was halfway down the steps when one of them turned.

"Don't move. Hands up." The Greek's voice was hard.

The two men obeyed slowly and wordlessly, their faces registering surprise.

Nanos went down the steps, his Skorpion trained on them. As they raised their hands, one of them glanced at the ship's intercom on the wall behind him.

"Play hero, play dead," Nanos warned.

One of them wanted to play hero. He dived for the intercom. Nanos pumped 7.65mm slugs into his back. The bullets were small but effective. The man spun over backward and dropped. Dead was for real.

The other man dived for Nanos. One steely hand grabbed his firing wrist, the other clenched at his neck, the thumb driving into the Greek's throat. Nanos heard a soft thud. The grip on his neck and arm tightened sharply, then fell away. Bubbles of blood gurgled from the man's lips and drooled down his chin. He fell forward onto his face. Nanos moved neatly out of the way, massaging his neck. Hayes's knife was buried to its hilt in the dead guy's back.

"I needed the practice," Hayes boomed from the gallery overhead. "Wipe it off for me, will ya?"

"Try to be a nice guy and look what happens," said Nanos. "Let's move ass."

Hayes led them up the companionway into the midship deckhouse. The long empty corridor was lined with a half-dozen cabin doors. Doors at both ends led to the deck outside.

"Officers' quarters," said Nanos.

"Let's clean it out," said Hayes, "then go for the bridge."

"You boys can handle this," Lopez said. "The crew's quarters are up front in the bow. When we go for the bridge, they're going to pour out of there. I'll take a walk up there and give them something to answer for from behind."

Without waiting for an answer, Lopez started up the corridor for the outside door.

"Lopez, you're nuts! You'll never get past the bridge without being spotted!" Nanos called.

"No sweat, man. The last thing they expect is for us to be on board. If anyone sees me, he'll think I'm a sailor."

The Latin smile flashed again. Lopez disappeared.

Hayes took up position at the far end of the corridor. Nanos tapped softly on the first door, then tried the handle. It opened. The cabin was empty. He went to the next.

At the third door he heard footsteps and a muffled

voice. He kept himself out of sight against the wall. A man in an undershirt peered out into the corridor. He ran into the steel barrel of the Skorpion machine pistol pressed into his forehead between his eyes.

"Don't move, don't say a word, and you'll live," Nanos snarled. He moved forward into the cabin, the barrel of his gun pushing the man back.

But this one didn't want to play, either. He threw himself into the corridor away from Nanos's gun. Hayes turned from the door and fired. What the Skorpion lacked in stopping power, it made up in speed. Bullets tore through guts. The man reached for a fire alarm on the corridor wall. Hayes fired again. The man's face disappeared in a red mask of splattered flesh. His hand wavered inches from the alarm. Then he death-gripped the lever as he collapsed.

The alarm went off.

Hayes and Nanos tore down the corridor toward the door to the deck, ditching their Skorpions. It was time to bring out the Commandos and have some heavy 5.56mm action.

"I'll cover this door and get them as they come in the other end," Nanos told Hayes. "You get out of here and circle around."

Outside, the daylight was torn by the howl of the alarm. Hayes raced around the deckhouse and edged past the lifeboat rack.

Four sailors were racing from the bridge. One carried a fire extinguisher. Hayes ducked back against the wall as they disappeared into the deckhouse.

Two more men appeared outside the upper level of the bridge. They were armed with automatic rifles. They saw Hayes.

NANOS WAITED at one end of the corridor inside the deckhouse. He didn't wait long.

The door at the other end opened, and the first of the four sailors burst in. He stopped, wide-eyed, when he saw the body leaking blood on the corridor floor. He wasn't looking for that. He was looking for fire. Nanos gave it to him. Firepower. A few 5.56mm rounds ripped open his chest.

The three men behind him kept coming, stumbling over each other, pushing farther into the corridor. They didn't know they should stop. It was like slapstick comedy. But the bullets weren't funny. Nanos slapped autofire into the second sailor. His gore blew back in his buddy's face. Nanos kept firing. The next one dropped. One to go. The Colt stopped firing. Nanos squeezed.

Nothing.

The mag was empty.

THE TWO MEN on the bridge raised their rifles at Hayes. The merc delivered a burst of autofire and ran for the front of the deckhouse where a bulkhead gave cover. Bullets pinged off the steel wall of the deckhouse by his head and slammed into the bulkhead. He could hear Nanos's autofire inside the deckhouse behind him. Then it stopped. Hayes turned. A sailor was running out. Hayes fired. The man fell back inside.

Nanos jammed a full mag into the Commando as the sailor ran for his life. Then the sailor came flying back in. This time he was dead.

Hayes filled the doorway. It sounded like all hell had broken loose outside.

"Take the roof of the deckhouse and throw some lead in the back windows of the bridge," said Hayes. "I'm going to keep them busy with these." He patted the tear-gas grenades on his belt. "If we're lucky, we'll get some covering fire from Lopez."

"If Lopez was lucky, we'll get some covering fire," Nanos shot back as he ran for the ladder that led to the deckhouse roof.

LOPEZ WAS LUCKY. He held his Colt Commando vertically below waist level as he took a nonchalant stroll past the bridge to the forecastle deck at the bow of the ship.

He got as far as the hatch when the alarm went off.

Throwing himself into a run, he reached the forecastle deck in five easy paces. There wasn't much cover except for some waist-high piles of coiled rope. The rope was as thick as a man's arm. It would do. He threw himself behind it.

The chatter of autofire came from the deckhouse where he had left Hayes and Nanos. Two men stood outside the bridge at the top of the stairs and fired their rifles in that direction. Lopez ran a line of autofire across the front of the bridge. One froze and fell down the stairs. The other jumped back inside.

The door to the crew's quarters opened below him. Three men armed with AK-47s headed for the midship action. Lopez crouched low and aimed. Someone on the bridge found him first.

He was a lousy shot, but the autofire ricocheted off the metal deck a foot in front of him. He dived for cover. Bullets thudded into the thick coils of rope. He looked and saw blood on his left shoulder.

That pissed him off. It was only a flesh wound. But it was the same shoulder that had been shot off in Africa a few wars ago, the one that Lee Hatton had sewed together. Lee had saved his life, and Lopez was thankful for it. He was going to kill the mother who messed around with his left shoulder.

He swung out of cover and sent hot lead winging across the bridge. The three sailors had already made it inside. The windows shattered. The roof of the bridge suddenly exploded. Lopez knew it wasn't his rifle that did that.

GLEN BEAM WAS ON THE BRIDGE with the captain and navigator of the *Sally Queen*, dreaming about money when the fire alarm went off. His daydreams blew up with a boom of reality. Red lights started running up and down a control panel as if they wanted to escape. Fire on a ship carrying a couple of tons of rifles, ammunition and a missile was no joke. If the ship went, they'd be vaporized. Beam included. But Beam had a helicopter. The others could fend for themselves if they had to.

The captain was shouting orders into the intercom. He had no illusions, either. His sailors weren't going to be too happy trying to put out a fire on a floating bomb. He ordered two of his officers to make an appearance with automatic rifles to back up his orders.

The two officers left the bridge house and got as far as the outside deck.

Beam watched from inside. It was a nightmare.

Giant red flowers bloomed across the chest of the second man out. He dropped his rifle and fell forward down the steps.

The first one started firing at an enemy no one could see. There were more noises rising above the honk of the fire alarm. The sound of bullets. A lot of them.

The first officer jumped back inside.

The captain spotted Lopez as the merc dived for cover on the bow of the ship. He shouted at the two remaining officers. The door to the crew's quarters opened onto the main deck below Lopez, and three crewmen made a dash for the bridge as the bridge returned covering fire.

The three crewmen had made the lower level of the bridge house and raced upstairs when the windows blew in. Everyone dived for cover in a rain of shattered glass. The first officer crumpled in a corner, his face bloody, his eyes dead.

Then the roof blew.

The frantic baying of the now decapitated alarm siren stopped.

The sailors and captain were returning fire to the bow

of the ship through the shattered windows, pinning down the adversary behind the coil of rope. The back windows shattered, and another downpour of glass shards drenched them.

Beam decided it was time to go.

The sailors crouched, returning sporadic blind fire out the windows. Beam sidled over to the companionway and began moving down. He hadn't figured out how he was going to get from the deckhouse to his helicopter parked on the wide stern of the ship. But he had a Mauser pistol and a couple of Diego's grenades in his pocket to help him out.

Beam had done a lot of things in his career, and someone else's death was pretty much inconsequential to him. But he'd never found himself in the middle of a shoot-out before. And the closest he'd ever come to the mad minute of war was at the movies.

He figured he'd just have to rely on luck. Then it came to him. He needed to create a diversion. It was an inspired flash. The controls to the electronic doors covering the cargo hatches sparkled with broken glass in front of him. He pressed the buttons.

He quickly descended the companionway to the lower level of the deckhouse. He locked the door that led to the deck outside. Then he pulled out his Mauser and turned back up the companionway.

The captain was on his way down as Beam went up. Beam shot him in the face. The sound of autofire from outside was rising to a crescendo. Shells from the sailors' guns danced around the bridge. The captain flew back against the companionway, then bounced down like a stiff on a playground slide.

Beam backed down quickly. He took one of the grenades from his pocket and pulled the pin with his teeth. Just like in the movies. And in the movies they held it for a count of five before throwing it. But Beam had never thrown a grenade before. Like hell he'd hold it. He threw it up the companionway onto the bridge as if it were burning his hand off. Then he backed himself into a corner. He had an instant nightmare that one of the crewmen upstairs would see it bouncing along the floor and throw it back down.

He waited, his hands over his ears, his heart pounding against his chest. Five seconds seemed like eternity.

Then it blew.

Beam took his hands away from his ears.

The rifle fire outside was dying. The rifle fire from above was dead.

He looked at the companionway.

Blood was splashing down the first steps like water over a falls.

NANOS STAYED LOW as he raced along the roof of the deckhouse. The smokestack shielded him. He saw the windows along the back of the bridge shatter in giant crystal spiderwebs as Hayes shot at them. Nanos pulled the pin from his grenade, counted and tossed it with a gentle underhand. It landed on the roof, bounced once, stopped and blew. The radio antennae careened and fell. Pieces of the siren flanked down onto the deck of the ship. The sound of autofire rose above the fast-dying shrieks of the alarm.

Pinned by Hayes and Lopez from two directions, the men inside the bridge returned blind, sporadic fire that went wild, pinging off the metal superstructures. They were caged. Now was the time to smoke them out.

Hayes was shooting the glass out of the windows. Nanos pulled a tear-gas grenade from his belt.

Then the bridge house blew up.

Shards of thick glass flew outward, leaving yawning holes. Rifle fire died from inside. Hayes's and Lopez's return fire became hesitant, then stopped replying to the silence. A strong wind blew across the ship, taking smoke from the bridge house out to sea.

The silence was terrible. More terrible than the noise of battle.

Nanos climbed down the ladder and walked around the side of the deckhouse where Hayes waited, pressed against the side of the ship.

"Something blew up in there. You figure they're all dead?"

Hayes shrugged. "I dunno. You wanna go in and ask?"

Nanos looked across the deck. The bridge was separated on all sides by a clear space.

"Cover me," he told Hayes. "Once I get across there, they can't shoot unless they stick their heads out the windows and fire straight down. I'll try the lower door and see how far I can get."

Hayes set his Commando on 3-round bursts and ran a line of fire across the gaping windows of the bridge. Nanos sprinted across the open deck and crammed himself tight against the wall of the deckhouse. He had a break. The ship's walls were made of metal. No one could fire through them. He could hear the rounds from Hayes's Commando ricocheting in the bridge above him. Other than that, it was dead quiet.

He moved forward to the door that led to the lower level of the bridge and tried the handle. It was locked.

There was only one thing left to do. Go up the companionway and in the front door.

He moved around the corner of the deckhouse, staying flush to the wall until he came to the foot of the companionway. Lopez had clued in and was giving cover from the other direction. Nanos climbed. Step by step. He didn't breathe. His finger and the metal trigger on his Commando were one instrument. His body was reaction. He spoke only death.

His head came up level with the floor of the bridge house, and he saw a body slumped inside the door. The body might once have been a man. Man meets grenade. Neither survives.

Suddenly Nanos knew it was all over. He breathed out and went up quickly. As a last precaution he doubled over at the top steps and threw himself across the doorway, aiming his Commando in a firing arc across the inside of the bridge. He didn't have to fire. He saw carnage.

Hayes and Lopez were still sawing away on either side of him with short bursts of autofire. Nanos stood up with his gun in his hand and waved it high over his head. The autofire stopped.

Hayes was the first up the steps.

"No more trouble with these guys," said Nanos. Neither merc wanted to walk into the room. It was running an inch deep in blood.

Hayes looked over the scattered mass of limbs and bodies that had once been men. They were really chewed up. None of them had a recognizable face. But one thing was missing.

The one thing Hayes was looking for most.

Blond hair.

"Beam. He's not here," the black man said.

Then they heard Lopez shout.

He was running past the bridge house toward the stern of the ship. Nanos and Hayes knew instantly. They ran for the helicopter just as the quickening sound of the rotors thudding in the air reached them.

Hayes and Nanos tore down the companionway and past the midship deckhouse. Lopez was already halfway down to the stern when the small H-23 Raven two-seater lifted off the end of the ship and hovered delicately in the air.

Lopez went down on one knee and raised his Commando.

The bullets hit the helicopter in the front windshield and bounced off the bulletproof glass. He held his aim up and tried for the delicate rotor hub. The helicopter rose up higher. Hayes and Nanos added their firepower.

The blond man inside was fiddling frantically with something as he pulled the gears into line. Then he threw something from the copter.

Something the size of a handball.

It winged across the stern of the *Sally Queen* and disappeared down the open hatch door into the hold.

It was a grenade.

The hold was filled with ammunition.

The ship was a bomb. It was going to go off.

The helicopter lifted off in reverse and away from the ship.

Lopez dived at the hatch door.

Spread-eagled in the air, he disappeared into the hold.

Nanos and Hayes heard the dampened thud of an explosion.

Nanos fired his Commando at the disappearing helicopter, firing until the mag was empty, and then he kept squeezing the trigger as the helicopter grew smaller over the Pacific waters. His rifle was empty, but he kept squeezing, hoping for more bullets to stop the helicopter.

He squeezed tears from his eyes.

He felt Claude Hayes's strong hand gripping his shoulder and from a far distance heard Hayes's voice.

"Okay, soldier, okay. It's okay."

The hand gripped tighter. Lopez was dead.

Nanos broke. A cry of sorrow stretched from his lips. He dropped to his knees. The useless rifle fell from his hands and clattered on the steel deck.

8

Bishop veered south and headed toward the blue expanse of the Pacific Ocean. An invisible line ran along the green landscape below, curling in and around volcanoes, crossing rivers and lakes. It was the Nicaragua–Costa Rica border. Sandinista antiaircraft batteries strung along the frontier were visible as small specks of brown in the surface relief below.

Bishop noticed Barrabas on the seat beside him, studying the ground below.

"That represents a lot of airspace I don't want to stray into."

Barrabas looked up.

"Not even with oil-company markings," he said, chewing on his cigar. "ETA?"

"Less than half an hour."

Barrabas raised his binoculars and rolled the focus to infinity. At maximum cruising speed of 150 mph, the chopper was soon well out over the water. Far ahead, the *Sally Queen* came into view, floating like a speck of ash on the surface of the Pacific.

In the fuselage behind him he heard the radio beep and Beck's voice replying. Beck poked his head into the front seat.

"Colonel, it's Hayes. The *Sally Queen* is secure but...." Beck stopped.

"Who?" Barrabas could see it on Beck's face. All he needed was a name.

"Lopez."

"Geez."

Lopez. The man was a good fighter. He wondered how Lee was going to take it. She had sewn him back together once in an operation in an African witch doctor's hut. It saved his life then. So now he bought it.

Barrabas forced his thoughts away. It was war. They had more battles to fight. When it was over they could talk about Lopez. And feel the sorrow.

When it was over. His blood quickened, and turned to anger. Add Lopez to the list. Another score to settle.

"Something else, Colonel," Beck started again. "Someone got away in a helicopter. They think it was Beam. There was a boat due to rendezvous with the *Sally Queen* in five hours. Hayes gave us the coordinates and Billy Two's figuring it out. But the helicopter might have warned them."

Barrabas got up and squeezed from his seat into the cabin behind. Billy Two was working over a chart. Lee did quick calibrations on a pad, efficient, businesslike, betraying no feelings about Lopez.

Barrabas turned to Beck.

"Radio Hayes and Nanos that we'll go for the rendezvous boat first. Tell them to clean up on the ship and we'll come back for them."

He crouched beside Lee Hatton. Billy Two had marked the position of the *Sally Queen* on the chart in front of him, and the series of X's joined by circles and lines marked the rendezvous point and the position of the boat an hour earlier. Billy Two pointed to an X.

"It was arriving at the rendezvous forty miles off the coast in four hours. Let's say it was going full out or almost full out. It had to be, because to get to the rendezvous at, let's say fifteen knots, it would've been here when it broadcast." Billy Two pointed to a second X. Between the two was a circle. "So it's about here now."

"A hundred miles northwest," said Lee. "That's if it

hasn't turned around to hightail it for wherever it came from once the helicopter warned it."

"And where did it come from?" asked Billy Two, staring hard at the chart. "Nicaragua?"

Barrabas studied the map.

The long straight coastline of the Marxist country stretched to the northwest where it met El Salvador, broken only by the Gulf of Fonseca.

"Not Nicaragua," Barrabas said. It didn't make sense.

The Sandinista government didn't have secure borders because of the rebel *contras* who attacked from bases in Honduras and Costa Rica. But the Sandinistas had complete control of their own countryside. And the seacoast. Their control was so good, according to Jessup's information, that they were supplying their villagers with arms. Only popular governments armed their own people. Whatever enemy the SOBs were dealing with was no friend of the Sandinistas. And the Sandinistas had Nicaragua clenched in an iron fist.

The boat they were going after now didn't come from Nicaragua. It came from somewhere else.

Barrabas studied the map. There was something Lopez had said once about forgery. "The best place to hide is the most obvious place." Then he saw it.

"There." Barrabas stabbed his finger at the map. "The Gulf of Fonseca."

It was a twenty-mile-wide body of water surrounded by swampland and bordered by three countries, none of which got along with the others: El Salvador, Honduras and Nicaragua. It was one of the most militarized pieces of ocean in the world. And the scene of some major arms trafficking, with the covert operations of any one of a half-dozen countries supplying weapons to any one of a half-dozen warring armies.

It was the best place in the world for a secret force to

bring weapons into Latin America. Right in the middle of everyone else's operation. It was perfect for whoever was behind this operation. Jessup was right. This could turn into the war of all against all.

But first they had to take the rendezvous boat.

Barrabas stepped back into the front seat. "Thirty degrees northwest," he told Bishop.

The pilot lined the helicopter up against coastal reference points and turned. Despite the full-out cruising speed, earth and ocean a mile below arched by with agonizing slowness.

An hour later they saw it: a forty-foot fishing boat. If it was the boat they were looking for, it had been warned. It was going full out to the northeast. Straight toward the Gulf of Fonseca.

"Think that's them?" Bishop asked.

"Let's go down and find out."

"Buzz 'em?"

Barrabas nodded.

Bishop brought the BK-117 down slowly and did a flypast off the port side of the boat.

They were answered by rifle fire.

"Not nice," said Barrabas. Any lingering doubts about who they were after were gone.

Bishop took the helicopter back up and out of range. The SOBs went into action.

O'Toole and Lee tore the cover off the Belgian MAG and fed in a fifty-round disintegrating link belt. The MAG was a good gun for the job ahead. Mounted on a tripod secured to the helicopter's metal floor, it had a range of a mile at a thousand rounds a minute.

Barrabas laid a series of different grenades on the floor of the cabin. He screwed an SMK-RFL-4ON smoke grenade onto the barrel of an M-16 and shoved a ballistite round mag into the breech. Using the Mecar system with live ammunition with rifle grenades was a lot more convenient. But the dud ballistite round gave him twice as much range.

And they'd need all the range they could get.

In boat versus helicopter, the boat usually won. A helicopter has a lot of maneuverability. But a boat could take a lot more damage before it ran into trouble. If the helicopter took a hit in any one of a number of delicate and vulnerable places, it was game over.

Barrabas wanted to drop a couple of minutes of white smoke cover onto the deck of the boat. He had to get within three hundred yards to do it, even with the ballistite round. The helicopter was an easy target from that distance, and the BK-117 didn't come equipped with armor plating. Bishop had a big job ahead of him. To keep the helicopter twisting and turning and out of fire.

Barrabas took a second M-16 and attached an M-203 40mm grenade launcher under the forestock. It gave him the same range as the ballistite round on the smoke grenade. He snapped a mag of 5.56mm rounds into the Armalite. The launcher was independent. He had automatic rifle to back it up. He finished by tucking 40mm offensive concussion projectiles into his belt.

Bishop brought the helicopter down, maintaining level flight attitude until his cruise speed equaled his descent speed. Then he lowered the nose into descending attitude—which was also defensive attitude.

The blade and tail rotor and transmission shafts on the underbelly were the most delicate parts. To go in on an attack, it was necessary to protect these parts by keeping the nose down and going in headfirst. That meant the pilot had to take it in the face. The bullet-proof glass deflected the autofire.

It still wasn't any fun. And the closer the helicopter came, the less likely it was that the bubble would stay bulletproof.

When Bishop had the BK-117 at a thousand feet, he leveled into a cruise, picked up speed and sailed toward the boat.

Bullets pinged off the windshield.

On the deck men armed with automatic rifles ran from the cabin to the bridge. The canvas roof was ripped off, and the ugly steel snout of an M-60 appeared.

Bishop rolled the helicopter out beyond the half-mile range and descended to seventy-five feet AGL. The Belgian MAG gave them over a three-hundred-yard lead. Barrabas thanked Silver John silently. It would probably mean the difference between victory and defeat.

Bishop turned the helicopter parallel to the boat and raised the nose.

"Go for it!" Barrabas flicked his cigar out the open window. The snout of the M-16 followed.

Lee Hatton pulled the side door of the fuselage open. The MAG made its appearance. O'Toole swiveled the barrel at the boat, his finger stroking the cold steel trigger. He pressed. The MAG spat 7.62mm rounds of killpower.

From that distance, death was silent.

The man behind the M-60 on the bridge flew back into the air, then sailed out over the deck and into the water. O'Toole kept his finger on the trigger as Lee fed bullets. The man at the controls caught lead and slumped against the instrument panel.

The helicopter passed over the boat. Autofire still followed them. Bishop pulled up the collective and pedaled torque hard to swing the chopper into a hairpin turn.

Billy Two and Barrabas sent M-16 fire back across the boat as O'Toole swiveled the MAG. The barrel was already red-hot. Lee grabbed the detaching handle, pulled it off and with the other hand had a new barrel ready to insert.

The helicopter went back for more, bearing down as Bishop twisted the throttle and gave it maximum rev. This time he pulled off along the side of the boat. Billy Two raked the deck with his M-16 fire while O'Toole drew a line of bullet holes along the side of the boat, taking out the portholes.

A man firing from the cabin door fell back, the door falling shut behind him.

Bishop pulled the nose up and spun the helicopter around. He lowered the nose like a bull going in for a charge.

They were still getting return fire from inside the cabin through the broken portholes.

Barrabas peered down the graduated-leaf sight on the grenade launcher on his M-16.

Bishop ran the bird over the surface of the water again.

Barrabas held his eye tight along the sight, gauging for helicopter movement and wind. He fired.

The projectile tore across the water, black and hard. Death knocked. A direct hit through the open porthole. The explosion blew debris out the windows. O'Toole gave a wild cheer.

Then Billy Two fired the smoke grenade as the helicopter passed above the boat. It exploded on the deck into a column of thick white smoke.

Bishop hairpinned the helicopter around again. From fifty feet AGL he decreased the collective with a slightly rearward cyclic. The nose of the bird stayed up. He continued with down collective and back cyclic to decrease his ground speed, bringing the helicopter in an arc over the smoke. Then he brought the cyclic forward and increased the collective.

It was a delicate maneuver requiring a high degree of coordination of all the controls to do a quick stop.

Once over the boat, he held the craft in a hover above

the smoke cloud blowing off onto the water. O'Toole and Lee had the side door open and ropes down. Lee was the first one out, rappelling down the rope twenty feet onto the deck in the cone of wind rushing up from the copter blades. O'Toole was next. Before he reached the ground he could hear Lee covering him by throwing autofire through the thick white smoke at the cabin door.

The smoke cover lasted barely two minutes. By then, O'Toole, Lee, Billy Two and Barrabas were on deck. Bishop backed the helicopter away.

A silence stretched tight around the boat as the smoke blew away on the ocean winds. The sides of the cabin were scorched and chipped from bullets, the deck slippery with spent shells. One man lay dead at the cabin door. Another sprawled above the steering wheel.

Lee was at the cabin door, which swung lightly with the movement of the boat on the water. Barrabas moved in beside her. He gave her the okay.

With the top of the barrel of her Armalite against the edge of the door, she swung it back and open. Barrabas went in running low with O'Toole behind.

The concussion grenade had done its damage in the narrow space. A body was sprawled flat, most of the chest blown away. The dead man's hand still clutched a broken AK-47.

Ahead of them, a corridor led into the bow of the boat. A pair of feet trailed out of the corridor. Barrabas knelt and touched the man's neck. There was no pulse.

He turned back to look at Lee Hatton and O'Toole.

"No prisoners," he said.

Then he heard the sound of a rifle click behind him.

Wood splintered and tore in a wide arc as Barrabas sprayed M-16 autofire. He flattened himself on his stomach and kept lead death pouring into the corridor. The sound of screams rose above the automatic-rifle fire. An AK-47 flew from a broken door and landed in the corridor. Barrabas stopped firing.

A foot kicked open a door. It was the head. A young man emerged slowly and cautiously, his hands up, his body hunched forward, and his shoulders tense and high, as if he expected bullets to rip him in two at any moment.

Barrabas could see the terror written on the man's face.

"You cooperate, you have nothing to fear," Barrabas told him in Spanish.

The man came slowly down the corridor to the cabin and stepped over the body of his colleague. He was young, his dark features indicating Indian blood. A dark, wet stain stretched from his crotch down the leg of his pants.

"Sit." Barrabas motioned to a chair with his rifle.

He held the steel point of the M-16 barrel against the man's forehead. The prisoner sucked in his breath and froze in terror. He waited for his brains to splash against the wall.

"There are others?" Barrabas asked.

The man shook his head quickly.

"No, señor. Todos muertos."

"You answer my questions, then you live. If you lie, you die," the colonel told him slowly and clearly. "Understand?"

The young man nodded and swallowed. His eyes became eager. It seemed a fair exchange for his life.

"Yo contesto todo," he said, stammering. He'd answer everything. Gladly.

"Who are you working for?"

"Some men. I do not know. They come to my village, Chirilagua, where my brother has this boat." The man's eyes swept over to the body sprawled on the floor of the cabin. "They give us much money to make this delivery to them."

"Where?" Barrabas demanded.

The prisoner hesitated. His eyes lowered.

Barrabas grabbed his hair and jerked the man's head up.

"Where?" he demanded again. He shoved the barrel of the Armalite into the man's temple.

The prisoner whitened with fear.

"Gulf of Fonseca," he cried, his voice cracking. Barrabas let go of the man's head. "We go to the Punta de Amapala. Some men meet us there, take the boxes from the ship and give us more money."

"And when do they expect you?"

"Tonight. After darkness. They will meet us with trucks to take away these things we bring them."

"Where do they take them?"

"I do not know." Again the prisoner's eyes moved down as he answered. Barrabas pushed the rifle barrel into the man's temple until he winced, his head squeezed between the wall and tubular death. Barrabas squeezed until his knuckles whitened.

The prisoner's eyes grew wide with desperation.

"No, no!" he said, panicked. "They tell us nothing! But in the village they are seen landing with helicopters like you, but bigger. But that is all! I do not know who these men are!"

Billy Two walked into the cabin.

"No charts, nothing." He wiped his hands on his pants. They were bloody from throwing the bodies overboard. "Bishop's bringing in Nanos and Hayes."

"Show him the map, Billy." Barrabas motioned toward the prisoner.

Billy Two unfolded the plasticized chart of El Salvador and handed it to the colonel.

Barrabas lowered his rifle and put the map in front of the prisoner.

"Show us where you land the boat. And where the helicopters land."

"Here is my village." The prisoner pointed to a spot inside the Punta de Amapala, a peninsula that jutted out at the northwest mouth of the Gulf of Fonseca. "We land the boat here." He pointed to a spot several miles up the coast of El Salvador. "There is a long dock there. Many rich people once kept their boats there. All around there were great houses for these people. The guerrillas have burned the houses. Now the rich no longer come. So we meet the men there."

"And the helicopters. Where do they land?"

The prisoner examined the map again. "There is a road from the dock along the shore where the big houses were. It is a kilometer away. Here." He pointed on the map. "At the end of the road."

Barrabas took the map and folded it.

"Okay, Billy, tie him up," he ordered. "Let's get this boat going again so we can make that rendezvous."

A HALF HOUR LATER, the BK-117 was overhead with Nanos and Hayes rappelling down onto the deck of the boat. Bishop took the copter out in a hover over the water a hundred feet off. Beck dropped the supplies in three bundles out the doors. They floated on the surface of the water like corks. Hayes and Nanos had barely hit the deck before they were stripping down to the wet suits they'd worn under their fatigues and putting on flippers. A few minutes later they had the three bundles at the side of the boat as O'Toole and Billy Two lifted them up over the gunwales.

The helicopter went up and disappeared in the direction of Costa Rica. Once again Bishop went back to being the pilot of an oil-company helicopter, going in for rest and fuel.

O'Toole and Lee started unloading the supplies of ammo and rations. Nanos checked out the engine while Hayes took the controls on the bridge. The boat vibrated as the engines revved and Hayes put it in gear.

The boat plowed through the water in the direction of the Gulf of Fonseca. Barrabas stood on the bridge beside Hayes looking ahead.

They were closing in.

And going straight to hell. El Salvador was the belly of the beast.

"You figure we'll make it in there without being seen?" Hayes asked.

"Depends," said Barrabas. "It depends on who's been paid not to look."

9

The warm Pacific waters of the Gulf of Fonseca rolled up over white sand beaches, and the beaches led to sprawling lawns. Once manicured, they now grew wild in a profusion of tangled bushes, saplings taking hold after the rains, and gardens gone to seed. The charred beams of a great burned-out house stood out against the night sky, silhouetted by the dim light beyond.

The abandoned gardens continued behind, bordering once elegant walkways and patios, to a long stretch of clay tennis courts. Oil lanterns glowed around the perimeter, turning a dozen men with rifles into the flicker of ground shadows. In the center of the circle of lights were two ancient transport helicopters, their cargo doors open and waiting.

Rafael Cruz wiped the grease off his hands with an old rag and stepped out of one of the helicopters.

"Put the cover back on," he ordered. A man with a wrench scrambled to obey. A piece of the metal floor was shoved over the dark hole that held the helicopter's guts, and the man began to screw it down.

Rafael walked away from the helicopter, still wiping his hands on the dirty cloth, anticipating what lay ahead. Jorge, his compatriot, was waiting silently in the other helicopter. Rafael walked toward him.

Rafael and Jorge were Cubans. The men with rifles were Salvadoran peasants hired from the nearby village and Americans Jeremiah had sent them from his settlement.

Rafael liked the Salvadoran peasants. They did what they were told. It wasn't like the Cuban army with its ideas about a democratic military. The lowest private had a say in what went on. There was no chain of command. No big boss except Marxist-Leninism.

The Salvadorans just did what they were told, when they were told. Except for the guerrillas, who were hopeless either way. Rafael didn't care anymore. He no longer worked for Castro. And he was going to be rich very, very soon. Meeting Jeremiah had been a lucky break. He thought about the money he had made—and the money he had yet to make—and was very happy.

Rafael had been a model soldier in the Cuban army. He distinguished himself as part of a supply chain to the Che Guevara guerrilla forces in Paraguay, and later by his performance in Angola and Ethiopia. He had thought of nothing but the struggle for world communism, of the historical necessity for the struggle against America and the capitalist exploiters.

So his leaders sent him to El Salvador. They had another war going on there—there were so many wars everywhere—and their soldiers in the FMLN needed training and advice. After all, the Americans were training the other side. It was only fair that the guerrillas should receive professional help, too. Rafael was glad to go and help advance the cause of Marxist-Leninist liberation.

So he and a fellow helicopter pilot—Jorge—were sent to teach the guerrillas how to fly helicopters. It was a silly idea, because the guerrillas didn't have any helicopters to fly. But they would obtain some, his superiors in Havana had said. First they had to know how to fly them. But how could he train people to fly helicopters unless he had helicopters to train them with? Rafael had asked. Ah, said the wise men in Havana, the principles of Marxist-Leninist struggle would guide him.

So he and Jorge came to El Salvador, lived in the mountains with the guerrillas, were wet in the rainy season and too hot in the dry season. They ate bad food, drank bad water and the Salvadoran women preferred the Salvadoran men, so the Cubans went without women, too.

Then they got lucky. One night they went into a little town controlled by the guerrillas. They sat in the little cantina, drank TicTac, the potent rum the Salvadoran peasants enjoyed, and sang Cuban songs—thirteen choruses of "Guantanamera."

Suddenly they noticed a shrunken little man at their table. He said he was Honduran. He told them he had an offer to make if they came to Honduras with him to meet someone. If they came, he said, they would make much money. Of course, they wouldn't be able to return, because as every soldier knows, the fate of deserters is death.

Rafael and Jorge had never thought about money before. Perhaps it was the TicTac swirling in their veins. Suddenly Marxist-Leninist principles didn't seem so much fun anymore. Money, thought Rafael, now *that* would be different.

The little man led them into Honduras, and they met a man called Jeremiah. At first the giant scared them. He was obviously a great leader of people because he was the leader of this great town. The settlement seemed every bit as Communist as Cuba did, but Jeremiah never talked about Marxist-Leninist principles. He talked about money.

He needed helicopter pilots. He mentioned a great deal of money. Enough to buy papers to go and live in Miami with other Cubans. And lots left over.

Rafael and Jorge switched allegiances. The giant had his pilots.

Rafael knew they were transporting weapons. They'd

brought in a load a month earlier. Then they sat around for a month waiting. Now they were to bring in one more load. Then they were free to go to Miami.

But for some reason the whole arrangement had been canceled two hours earlier. They just received a radio message to return to the settlement immediately.

This did not appeal to Rafael and Jorge for two reasons. First, one of the ancient helicopters needed some emergency repairs. Second, they didn't trust Jeremiah. They didn't believe he'd give them any more money when they returned, especially since he'd canceled the mission. Rafael and Jorge had seen the strange power Jeremiah had over his people.

So Rafael and Jorge changed their plans once again. Guatemala wanted helicopters. Rafael and Jorge would take the two they had, sell them in Tegucigalpa, and then go to Miami. As for the Americans and Salvadorans at the loading site, they were in for a big surprise.

They were going to be killed.

Jorge was waiting when Rafael arrived at the second helicopter.

"We are ready now, my friend." Rafael put his hand on Jorge's shoulder. Jorge was peeling a banana and popping pieces into his mouth. He looked up at Rafael.

"The end of our long journey. In a few days, Miami."

"*Sí*. Miami. And we will be rich men."

One of the Americans from Jeremiah's camp approached them, his rifle slung carelessly back over his shoulder.

"It ready yet?" the American whined.

Rafael looked at him. He still hated Americans.

"Come on, man. We were supposed to be out of here an hour ago. We don't like to keep Jeremiah waiting."

The Americans, thought Rafael, are always complaining.

"We have just finished," the Cuban explained. "We are putting the covers back on, and then we go. You can call everyone together, and we will board the helicopters in a minute."

"Fantastic." The American man turned and hurried away to collect the others. Rafael stared after him. He found these Americans so gullible. Friendly, but they believed anything.

Jorge's voice interrupted his thoughts.

"Miami," he said as if it were a dream. With his right hand he patted the canvas lump beside him. The canvas barely concealed the shape of a machine gun.

HAYES KEPT THE BOAT in international waters twelve miles offshore until they turned toward the coast just past the Nicaraguan coastal village of Corinto. Night fell quickly, and on the coast the conical outlines of sleeping volcanoes zigzagged up against the first stars appearing in the east.

The prisoner, Antonio, stood on the bridge between Claude Hayes and Lee Hatton, who translated from Spanish to English for Hayes's benefit. Hayes spoke Swahili and a half-dozen African dialects, but no Spanish. Antonio had warmed to his captors. He was being very helpful as he guided them to the exact spot inside the Gulf of Fonseca.

Hayes swung the boat past the Punta Condega on the Nicaraguan side of the entrance to the gulf, coming into Salvadoran waters due south of the Punta de Amapala. Occasionally, the dim light of an oil lamp would flicker from some peasant's isolated hut on the distant shore. They kept the running lights off, and as Hayes slipped the boat into the Gulf of Fonseca, he cut the engine to low cruise speed. It was barely a gurgling murmur along the surface of the water.

Nile Barrabas stood on the deck of the boat watching the shore coming closer, the curving mountains noticeable only because they were a more solid dark than the rest of the night. They'd taken what precautions they could to avoid detection, but Barrabas knew that if someone out there had radar or infrared detectors, it was all over. And despite Antonio's sudden cooperation, there was no guarantee they weren't being led into a trap.

"Aquí." There. Barrabas looked at the bridge and saw Antonio pointing to shore. Hayes turned the craft slowly and after a few minutes slipped the engine into idle. It drifted in toward the shore. Barrabas raised his passive night binoculars. He could see a dark pier looming out from the shore a half mile away.

The docking area looked deserted through the light-amplification binoculars, but they weren't much good for picking out people from the shrubbery and trees that began a hundred feet back from the shore.

He fingered his Canadian-made Browning HP pistol. One of his favorites. The 9mm parabellums were small but deadly up to eighty yards at a velocity of five hundred yards a second. It was one of the best handguns around. Barrabas screwed a silencer onto the end of it.

Around the boat the other SOBs checked out their gear. It was time for more of Silver John's stealth equipment. They attached flash suppressors to their Armalites and strapped Mecar rifle and polyvalent grenades to their waist belts. Billy Two slung his M-16 over his shoulder and handled his British L4A1 sniper rifle with the Startron nightscope. They were ready.

Nanos had the ten-foot reconnaissance boat inflated and over the side. Billy Two was climbing down the ladder. Barrabas turned back to Hayes, Lee and O'Toole. He'd briefed his soldiers and they knew their parts. None of them knew what the unexpected would be, and that was the part of war every soldier had to be prepared for the most. Barrabas gave them a silent look before hoisting himself over the side and descending into the reconnaissance boat.

Wordlessly, Billy Two let go of the line and Nanos began paddling the dinghy until they were caught by the waves. They'd dispensed with life preservers, lashings and harnesses. Either they'd make it or not. If they didn't, none of that would matter.

A chorus of waves rolled them quickly toward the dark shore. As the sandy beach grew closer, Barrabas watched through his binoculars. The beach was deserted. Barrabas ordered Nanos and Billy Two to shift their weight to the rear of the boat, then he dug his paddle into the water to keep the stern sideways to the waves.

A big white-crested roller caught up the bottom of the boat, pushing it in an easy glide over the last stretch. Before the wave had descended in its flight back to the ocean, Barrabas was over the side with the bowline. Nanos and Billy Two followed quickly.

"Low carry, move!" Barrabas whispered the order. They hoisted the boat out of the water and brought it up the beach in a low run.

There was a dead silence. Only the sounds of crickets and ocean breezes blowing onto the land's dry scrub.

The three mercs ran silently and quickly across the sand to the cover of the scrub forest a hundred feet beyond the shoreline. Barrabas turned his night glasses toward the pier, a quarter mile down the shore. The boat was still a few hundred yards out in the water.

"Can you get a sight on it from here?" Barrabas asked Billy Two.

The Indian nodded. He raised the sniper rifle to his shoulder and aimed toward the landing zone.

Barrabas stood and motioned to Nanos. The two of them slipped into the forest and moved quickly forward toward the pier, racing to get there before the boat did.

HAYES RAMMED THE GEARS OF THE BOAT into reverse to slow the forward motion as the boat cruised in alongside the wooden pier. When the boat stopped he cut the engines. He listened for noise from shore. There was none. O'Toole stood beside Antonio, gripping his Walther P-38. They waited.

Not for long. A spotlight beamed from the forest at the end of the pier, freezing the boat in its stark light, then sweeping across the deck and stopping on the bridge. The mercs squeezed back to hide their positions.

"Go!" O'Toole ordered in a whisper. He relaxed his hold on Antonio. The man stepped forward to the side of the boat and jumped onto the pier with a rope in his hand.

"We are here," he shouted in Spanish, busying himself by wrapping the rope around an iron ring. "And we have the guns."

A voice called back from the pitch blackness behind the glaring light. "Only you? Where are the others?"

"There, *señor*—they are there," Antonio said. He was trying to play it cool, giving a casual wave back toward the boat. But he got scared.

His eyes shifted and he flicked a nervous look over his shoulder. It was enough to alert whoever was standing there behind the light. Antonio knew it. He threw himself down onto the pier in a panic. Autofire ripped across the pier, skipping over Antonio's back and chunking into the bow of the boat.

A thousand feet up the beach, Billy Two's nightscope overdosed on the light from the spot. Billy Two was shooting blind. He drew a line on a few feet of space behind the light. Head level. He fired.

The man holding the light lost his brains. The spotlight dropped and smashed as the body rolled over onto the grass.

On board the ship, Hayes flipped a switch that threw on the boat's spot. Back to the original plan. This time the light was coming the other way.

Two men with automatic rifles aimed at the boat were clearly illuminated at the end of the pier. It caught them off guard. Where once they'd seen a boat, now they saw a blinding light. Like a revelation.

But the revelation was for Barrabas and Nanos, staked out in the scrub forest behind the pier.

Barrabas held the Browning HP straight out, his arm extended and steadying for recoil with his left. He fired. The silenced pistol coughed up three fast rounds.

The first man curved forward as his knees buckled beneath him. He went down dead.

The second had just raised his automatic rifle to lay a line of autofire back at the blinding light. Nanos's gun popped. The rifle fell from the man's hands as he died.

Hayes cut the light.

The night jumped back in to fill the gap, bringing with it the soothing sweep of waves rolling up the beach on the other side of the pier.

Barrabas strode forward onto the dock. Hayes, Lee and O'Toole came down from the boat as Billy Two jogged up from the beach.

Antonio still lay facedown and spread-eagled on the pier. The man was alive and shaking with fear.

Barrabas reached down and pulled him up.

"Antonio, I keep my word. We'll leave you here. We go to stop the men with the helicopters. When we finish we'll come back and release you. Then you can go free." Barrabas turned to Nanos. "Tie him up," he ordered.

The Greek hustled the prisoner back onto the ship.

Barrabas led the SOBs east in the direction Antonio had told them to go. The old road ran in front of the pier and along the beach for a short distance before turning slightly inland. Billy Two knelt and examined the gravel.

"Heavy truck. Recent."

Barrabas nodded. So far, Antonio's information was good.

They jogged a quarter mile, stopped and began walking in two groups of three on either side of the road, ready to slip into the forest at any sign of the enemy.

On the coastal side, overgrown lawns stretched out to beaches so white they glowed in the night. From time to time they passed the burned-out hulks of great houses the wealthy had deserted after the guerrillas left their fiery calling cards.

Two-thirds of a mile later the road turned. Barrabas motioned the SOBs into the covering bushes. The road ended at a stone wall where great iron gates hung lopsidedly. The guerrillas had called. They'd been blown off a long time ago. There were two sentries. They looked bored.

Barrabas crept forward, Billy Two crouched beside him.

"Go for it!" he whispered.

Billy Two raised the sniper rifle again. On the other side of the road Lee Hatton was doing the same thing. The two soft pops were indistinguishable noises among the night sounds of the wind in the forest. The sentries ceased to exist.

The six mercs poured through the gates in a low run, their rifles up. Ahead of them the blackened ruins of still another burned-out mansion stood silently.

Through the charred timbers of the roof they could make out a dim light coming up from behind.

Barrabas snapped out the orders.

"O'Toole, take Lee and Hayes and circle around to the right. Nanos, Billy—we go left."

The two attack parties separated in silent runs across the grass. When Barrabas came around the side of the destroyed house he saw the target.

The two transport helicopters were still parked on each side of what had once been clay tennis courts.

The courts were surrounded by burning lanterns. Two men chatted inside the loading door of one of the helicopters. At the side of the courts a dozen men stood talking. They carried rifles.

Barrabas motioned back to Billy Two and Nanos without taking his eyes from the scene in front of him. A rush of energy flooded him, and he could feel his hand tensing on the trigger of his M-16. It was the rush that came from homing in on the target, the danger of battle a split second away. The three mercs flattened themselves in the grass, keeping the barrels of their rifles up and aimed ahead.

BACK AT THE PIER another kind of action took place. Barely had the SOBs disappeared up the road away from the landing when a dozen dark figures slipped out of the forest and strode quickly up the wooden dock.

"Search the boat, Ricardo," the short one at the head of the party commanded one of the men. Ricardo motioned to two men behind him, and they quickly boarded the boat. The commander motioned to four others.

"Follow them up the road. If they turn back, you can kill them. Otherwise, wait for me." The four men disappeared up the road.

A minute later, Ricardo and his two comrades were pulling the struggling and terrified Antonio down the pier toward the land. The young man's hands were still tied behind his back and his mouth was gagged.

The commander pulled a knife from its sheath and with a savage tug slit the gag, allowing the prisoner to speak.

"Who were those men?"

Once again, desperate for his life, Antonio co-operated.

"Americans. I do not know. They search for the men who own the helicopters to destroy them."

"Who is their leader? I want a name."

"He is a colonel. They call him Barrabas. They came in a helicopter and took the boat. My brother was killed because he tried to run away."

"I know you," the commander's voice became deadly. "You are from the village. You and your brother and those others on the boat were bringing weapons to the men in the helicopters."

"Yes! No!" Antonio sputtered, his terror increasing. He shook his head madly in a vain effort at denial.

The commander turned and walked ten paces away before turning back to the terrified prisoner.

"In the name of revolutionary justice, the People's Army of El Salvador sentences you to death."

The commander nodded to the two men who held Antonio.

One twisted his arms up behind his back, forcing the man to his knees and pushing his head forward. The second pressed the barrel of a small pistol against his nape. The gun snapped and Antonio fell forward, his legs kicking out behind him. Blood jetted across the wooden planks of the pier in a long spurt.

The body was still.

The commander watched without moving.

"And the American soldiers?" asked one of the guerrillas. "Are they mercenaries?"

"They are mercenaries," said the commander. "And the revolutionary army has already announced the fate of mercenaries captured in our territory."

"They will die?"

"They will die." The commander turned and began walking quickly to the road. The others followed.

RAFAEL STEPPED OUT OF THE SECOND HELICOPTER, giving Jorge one last pat on his shoulder.

"In Miami, my friend," he said, referring again to their final destination, mouthing the words like a prayer.

"In Miami." Jorge gave him the thumbs-up sign and slipped his hands under the canvas tarpaulin beside him. He felt the cold steel of the machine gun's trigger and swung the barrel slightly.

Rafael called to the Americans gathered at the far side of the landing zone.

"Over here, *señores*." The group of men began walking toward the helicopters.

"What about the sentries and the men down at the pier?" the leader of the men called to Rafael.

"I will take care of them," Rafael called back, striding toward his own helicopter.

Jorge swung the barrel of the machine gun under the canvas until it was pointed at the group of men coming toward him. They were twenty feet away. He pulled the trigger.

The first bullets tore through the canvas on their death run into the flesh of the ignorant victims. Seven hundred rounds a minute. A river of lead.

Jeremiah's soldiers barely had time to register surprise before the bullets mowed them down. Their death screams flooded the air. The rapid fire of the machine gun chopped at the noise. The victims didn't try to use their rifles. They tried to run. But there was no escape.

Jorge calmly swept the machine gun back and forth. One by one in rapid succession the bodies of the fleeing men erupted in red gore. Some of them froze and died on their feet, collapsing into heaps of limp rags. Four of them made a run for it. Their screams died as their bodies hit the ground.

It took Jorge less than ten seconds to kill all of them.

The canvas over the hot barrel had just started to smoke.

Then Jorge heard bullets pinging off helicopter metal. What was going on? he wondered. How could anyone shoot back? He had just killed them all.

A bullet mashed his chest.

It was a Barrabas bullet.

Jorge screamed and flew back. He looked down at his body. He was covered with blood. He tried to stand, but he fell forward out the door of the helicopter with more bullets catching him as he hit the ground facedown. He was dead.

In his helicopter, Rafael sat at the controls watching the slaughter of Jeremiah's men. He slipped the key into the ignition and kept the engine at idle. He saw that most of them were dead. A couple were still running off toward the ruins of the house. He watched Jorge turn the barrel of the gun. The two running men dropped. Rafael turned away, no longer interested. He slipped in the clutch to engage the rotor. It started flapping against the wind, and the rush of air climbed up over the side of his helicopter. Then he heard another scream.

He slipped a quick glance over his shoulder. Jorge was standing up at the door of the other copter. He was drenched in blood. Rafael watched as Jorge wobbled out the door and fell flat onto the ground. Then he saw something that really scared him.

Soldiers with rifles. Streaming out of the night from every direction on the other side of the perimeter of lights. Panic revved up in his throat. He pumped the engine of the helicopter to maximum rpm.

Dust kicked up from the clay court outside the fuselage. They were firing at him. The panic clawed at his chest. He pissed himself. He tried to get the copter up in a maximum performance takeoff. But it was too late for Rafael.

Barrabas slammed an antitank rifle grenade onto the barrel of his M-16. He aimed down the graduated grid at the helicopter.

Rafael had it airborne; the chopper was a couple of feet off the ground. Barrabas pulled the trigger. Rafael almost had it in a climbing attitude when the explosion went off behind him. The helicopter shook violently. With a big bang it slammed back down onto the landing pad.

The Cuban was thrown back and out of the seat. He felt something warm on the back of his head. He knew it was blood. Soldiers were crossing the perimeter of lights now, hopping over the bodies of the massacred men. But Rafael still had his submachine gun. He picked it up and turned toward the soldiers coming toward him. His back was burning hot. He could barely move. He could smell something, too. Gasoline. The fuel tanks had ruptured. Rafael raised his submachine gun and aimed for the soldier closest to him. The one with the white hair and the face like hell.

He squeezed the trigger.

Bullets tore across his chest, pushing him back against the windshield. The cyclic stick forced itself up between his legs, doubling his agony. The SMG fired. Into the fuel tanks.

The force of the explosion threw Barrabas back and wiped his face with an instant sunburn. The helicopter was a ball of fire. Rafael's last horrible screams crawled from the flaming wreckage. Then it stopped. All Barrabas heard was the sound of greedy flames consuming flesh and plastic.

"You all right?" It was a cool, soft voice. Lee Hatton. She had her arm out to help him.

"C'mon." Billy Two had run up beside him and was also reaching out an arm. Barrabas didn't want help. He jumped, grabbing each of them by the arm and pulling them to the ground just as Rafael's SMG mag went off inside the fiery helicopter and sprinkled the air with shrapnel.

The miniexplosions died. The flames lit up the trees around the landing zone with an unholy glare, glinting off the pools of blood slicked on the grass around the bodies of the dead men. The flames were lowering quickly. There wasn't a lot to burn in a metal helicopter, except Rafael's charred corpse, sitting stiffly in the pilot's seat. It was still too hot to smell burning flesh. That would come soon enough.

Barrabas pushed himself up and surveyed the hellish scene as the other SOBs gathered at their leader's side.

He took a cigar out of his breast pocket and lit it.

"No prisoners." He blew out a ball of smoke.

"Dead end, Colonel," said O'Toole.

Barrabas was silent. He watched the flames die on the helicopter. The night began to close in.

"Maybe." He was silent again. "There's one more chance."

"The guerrillas," said Lee.

"The guerrillas. They'll know what we're looking for because they know the territory."

"Won't Uncle Sam love this," said Nanos grimly.

"That means making contact with Rosaria, the guerrilla leader," Lee added.

"Problem is—" Barrabas blew out another ball of smoke "—we gotta find her first."

A soft thud high in the overhead sky presaged the

bright glow of an unexpected flare. The landing zone lit up in a reddish light, and the descending flare sent mad shadows skittering along the ground. The sudden light glinted off faces and barrels of guns. There was no time to react. They were surrounded.

A small figure carrying an M-16 stepped forward. The tight fatigues betrayed a female figure.

"You need look no further, Colonel Barrabas, agent of American imperialism. I am Rosaria."

Guerrilla soldiers pushed into the clearing behind her. The amazon guerrilla leader lowered her voice and faced Nile Barrabas squarely.

"You fought a good battle, Colonel. But you are in the wrong war."

The guerrillas raised their rifles.

10

Shadows spread across the thousands of acres of farm-land that had been cleared from the Honduran jungle. The valley, lush and green from the rains, swollen with coffee and banana crops, sank into the half-light of evening.

The long line of workers left the fields and followed the road along the river to where the valley narrowed between two volcanoes. On one side of the river, cliffs jutted up to the high crater of Pentayan.

On the other side, a mile-wide plateau rose gently from the riverbanks to the slopes of Pentayan's sister, Quentoya.

On either side of the plateau, two great arms of cooled ancient lava ran from both of Quentoya's volcanic shoulders to the river like outstretched paws of a sleeping lion.

Cradled in the flat land between lay Jeremiah's New Society.

The long columns of workers trudged along the road and turned where the stream, flowing down the slopes of Quentoya, joined the river. They passed under a guard tower and through the gates of a high wire fence. The fence was topped with coils of sparkling razor wire. Black-uniformed guards closed the gates after them.

The women filed off through long, semicircular rows of narrow frame buildings to pick up their children at the school. The men walked to the communal dining hall at the wide central plaza that lay at the foot of

Quentoya's slopes. Soft music floated down over the camp from speakers mounted on columns along the edge of the central plaza.

The soothing melodies were carried by the warm breezes of dusk like perfume on the air, drifting faintly along the valley and wafting up the slopes of the volcano until they reached the open windows of a large house. At the window stood an enormous man. He watched his little empire.

Jeremiah's huge body filled the room. At seven feet, and with shoulders a yard across, he stood with the bulk of an upright piano. The span of his enormous hands was twelve inches, and their strength could crush a man's skull like an eggshell. He knew. He had done it once.

On this tropical evening, the giant's forehead was furrowed in discontent. The valley looked simple, prosperous and peaceful. Terror kept people in line, and death was a fine weapon.

The New Society. His empire. Soon it would be much bigger. He could hardly wait.

Outwardly Jeremiah was, as always, calm. Inside, he burned with fury. Only twice in his life had his anger got the better of him, and it had been fatal for those who had provoked it. He turned from the window.

The room had been built to suit Jeremiah's size. The ceilings were ten feet high, the furniture twice normal size. It was not only geared for the giant's comfort, but also was calculated to awe and overpower.

The thin blond man looked small, puny and lost in the gigantic sofa on which he was seated.

"It has taken fifteen years," Jeremiah said with forced calm, his eyes riveted on the little man on the sofa. Beam squirmed visibly. "Fifteen years to plan this. And everything has worked perfectly. Until today."

"So don't accuse me of nothing." Beam threw his hands into the air in a gesture of helplessness. The best way to handle Jeremiah was cool. He was having a hard time being cool. "I don't know who they were or where they came from. All I know is we were sailing along in the Pacific Ocean on the *Sally Queen* and all hell breaks loose."

Jeremiah stared hard at him with eyes like lasers. Beam pushed himself farther into the sofa and swallowed.

A pale man wearing the black overalls of Jeremiah's armed guard entered the room. Jeremiah turned his head slowly to the guard.

"The Costa Rican base will not transmit. No acknowledgment. No response." The man's voice was dull and monotonous.

Jeremiah shot Beam another look. Beam shrugged.

"Cancel the pickup on the Gulf of Fonseca and order them back to camp immediately. The senator arrives tomorrow. To visit our irrigation project," added the giant derisively. He paced and brooded a moment. Then he turned back to the guard. "We march tonight!"

Beam watched the guard leave the room slowly and deliberately, without a flicker of expression. Everyone here talked like zombies, moved like zombies. That was bad enough. But Jeremiah! Jeremiah thought he was God. The place gave Beam the creeps and he wanted out. Fast.

The giant turned back to Beam. In his hands he toyed with a cassette tape. He held it up. It looked like a book of matches between his two sausagelike fingers.

"Technology," said Jeremiah, "has been very useful. Follow me."

The giant led him from the room to a long deck that ran around the building. Below it, Quentoya's stream curled to the valley below. Jeremiah turned left, up some narrow stone steps, toward another wooden house built into the side of the volcano. Beam could hear the hum of machinery as they approached. Plastic pipes on stilts ran from the building and down the hill.

"We've come a long way since San Francisco and 1968, haven't we, Beam," said Jeremiah as they walked. "Who could have predicted then that our paths would be so entwined as they are today? And it all began so simply. Give people what they want. Tell them what they want to hear. When I discovered that, I discovered. . . ." Jeremiah paused to savor the words as he slipped the key into the door of the building. He looked at Beam. His look terrorized the man. "I discovered who I was. A savior of sorts. Or a gift. Yes, a gift. There are leaders and there are followers. I was to lead my followers to a better world. A New Society."

Jeremiah opened the door but turned before entering to look back down into the valley. Lights had come on, floating above the roofs of the buildings like little stars.

"My followers and I came here to create our own perfect world. We created all of this," he said, his voice rising, waving his arm across the vista that stretched below. "We released underground water from the volcano into this stream, which turned the dry creek in the valley into a river, and with the river we irrigated the land to make it fertile."

He paused, breathing in deeply, as if he were sucking up the landscape below.

"The secret to the success of New Society is water. I have taught my followers to worship it. With the greatest devotion. Come with me, Beam. I'll show you why."

Jeremiah swung back the door. In one quick glance Beam saw it all. Intake pipes from the mountain stream poured fresh water into two-story holding tanks buried into the floor. The holding tanks were connected to pipes that led to the settlement's drinking water.

"And this one, Beam, is yours," said Jeremiah as he moved easily and with familiarity along the gallery. The giant patted the lid of a small tank fastened above the holding tanks and connected by pipes. Jeremiah opened a valve on the pipes, and the contents began flowing out.

"Pentothal. For hypnotic control. The drug works gradually, as you know. Slowly it builds up in the body, lodging in fat cells, tranquilizing the mind, destroying the will, until...."

"They do what you want."

"Everything. You have supplied the chemicals. They have been quite useful!"

"And that one? What's that one?" Beam asked, pointing to another tank set off from the rest but also connected by pipes into the main water supply.

Jeremiah walked toward it. The steel tank came to the level of his waist.

"A few people are more resistant to the drug. As you know. And sometimes they feel upset by the perfection we have created here. They are eliminated." He patted the tank.

"The cyanide," said Beam. He knew. He had supplied it.

Jeremiah was silent.

"Come with me," he suddenly ordered, and set off quickly through the building, up steps to a second level. A large room looked out over the valley. At a long panel in front of the window lay the communications equipment and controls. Jeremiah slipped the cassette tape out of his pocket and pushed it into a player. He made adjustments on the panel. Red and green lights began playing up and down the controls, measuring the levels.

Gradually, Beam began to hear something. The beat of a drum drifting up from the valley, then many drums joining in together in a steady, terrible beat. The sound poured into the camp through the speakers along the central plaza. It began softly, then built higher, faster. Over the steady, thumping beat came the low sound of voices chanting, hundreds of them together, calling the name of their leader. *Je-re-mi-ah-Je-re-mi-ah.* Over and over in unison with the steady drumbeat.

Beam staggered back against a wall, horrified, unable to take his eyes off the insane man.

Jeremiah laughed, almost lightheartedly.

"Follow me, Beam," the giant cried, rushing from the room, down the stairs, and out the building.

Beam rushed after him, trying to keep up.

"So, Jeremiah, all I want is the money you owe me and some gas for my helicopter. It's your show from here on in."

"But I don't have my weapons yet," Jeremiah answered. He turned onto the steps that led down the slopes of the volcano to the central plaza.

"Come on, man. I kept my part of the bargain." Beam's imploring voice became breathless as they descended quickly.

"I will pay you when I am ready, Beam. Besides—" Jeremiah stopped briefly on the steps "—I want to share my adventure with you." He started down the steps again.

Beam could see dark shapes of people gathering in the central square at the bottom of the hillside. The voices chanting Jeremiah's name grew louder, harder.

"I don't want to share it. I want to go. Now."

"But you don't realize what it means, do you? In a few days, a few weeks at the most, I will control Central America."

"It's your game plan, man. Good luck with it. I just wanna get out of here. I got business affairs waiting. Come on. The money."

"Have patience. I have the feeling that you are afraid

of me. Of what I'm doing." Jeremiah stopped again on the steps. His smile glowed in the night. The smile said "Trust me"; the eyes called him a fool. The chanting became faster as the drumbeat quickened. They called for their leader.

"Man, I don't know what you're doing, and I don't care. Just don't drag me into it." Beam's voice was thin and worried. He felt closed in. He was a prisoner.

"Look!" Jeremiah roared and flung his hand out toward the plaza at the foot of the hill. The chanting and drumbeat had risen to a deafening crescendo.

Beam looked.

The plaza was filled with hundreds of men in black uniforms lined up in orderly rows. In front of them at intervals along the plaza, team leaders led them in drills. The chanting was punctuated with sounds of magazines injected, bolts pulled back, triggers cocked. The men moved their rifles in unison. Hundreds of women gathered around the shock troops. All of them chanted Jeremiah's name over and over.

In orderly groups, men and women holding little cups ran to a row of faucets set in a long trough at the edge of the plaza. They filled their cups and greedily drank the Pentothal-laced water.

"Control," said Jeremiah softly, his voice barely audible. The terrible chanting of his name filled the valley between the two volcanoes.

"My armies—" Jeremiah's voice broke in Beam's ear. He was leaning close, looking out over Beam's head, and pointing.

"One army, the one there on that side, a hundred men." He pointed to the left side of the plaza. "They will march on Salvadoran troop positions in El Salvador. The one next, they will go to destroy the guerrilla camp in the Morazán. The middle one I send against Honduran government troop positions and the American installations. Very close to us here. And of the last two, one will fight against the Nicaraguan *contras*, and the last will invade Nicaragua itself.''

Beam shuddered.

''You don't understand?'' Jeremiah's voice continued, soothing and reassuring. ''It's simple. Each of the five forces at war in this region will be attacked by unidentified forces. Each attacked force will undoubtedly think it is their enemy who attacked them.''

''And then?''

''And then everyone will go on the offensive. There will be total war. America will have to invade Central America to protect it from the Russians. It will have no choice. There will be a power vacuum. I have arranged to fill it. The senator who arrives tomorrow for a goodwill visit? I have owned this senator for years! Perhaps he will try to stop me. But by then it will be too late. To save his skin, he will have to save mine.''

The giant sighed wistfully, the steady, rhythmic chanting of his name calming him, removing the fury that had built up inside.

''You see, Beam, there has always been one problem with my New Society. It's not big enough. In order to make it truly perfect, I need a country. You will watch it being born.''

The color drained from Beam's face. It was going to be difficult for him to escape. And escape was all he thought about.

''At midnight tonight?'' He tried to submerge the fear in his voice.

''Tonight,'' Jeremiah said. He stretched out a comforting arm. ''Come. I will announce it to my army now. You will watch.''

Majestically, the giant man descended to the central plaza, where the mad chanting of his name rose to greet him.

BISHOP GUIDED THE HELICOPTER by the light shining off the ocean until the twenty-five-mile opening of the Gulf of Fonseca showed on his starboard side. Behind him in the cabin he could hear the squawks and static from Beck's radio and the sporadic clicking of a keyboard.

Beck's equipment—the radio and computer—didn't take up much room. With the radio tuned into shortwave, he could monitor one channel while the computer kept track of what was going on along the dial. Other occupied frequencies showed up continuously on the readout, with indication codes. The selection process was aided by programming. Beck had programmed Jessup's military codes into the machine and asked the computer to send back the emissions broadcast in those codes. The machine was very busy.

"The air is like alphabet soup out there," he shouted up to Bishop. "It's about as busy as the Philly Telephone Exchange." There were five identifiable armies in the vicinity, and it seemed that every camp and platoon was waving hello.

"Anything interesting?" Bishop called back over his shoulder. The computer wizard's face was lit up a ghostly blue from the light of his screen.

"Uh-uh. Just courtesy calls. Guys gossiping about who they laid last night and who they're gonna lay tonight. Fantasy stuff."

The computer automatically recorded all the coded broadcasts and automatically decoded them. This kept the machine busy deep in its chips. One by one Beck called up the decoded programs and read them. Then a number flashed rapidly on his screen. The code indicated priority.

Beck backfiled the message he was reading, punched in the number and pressed readout. Letters leapfrogged into sentences across the screen.

"Got some action."

Another number began flashing in the upper right corner of the screen. Again Beck's fingers tripped across the keyboard. He had barely finished it when a third number began flashing.

"What's happening?" Bishop could hear the sudden outburst of finger energy coming from behind him.

"Someone's using the codes we picked up in Costa Rica. And there's a lot of sudden action down there. They're sending out coordinates."

There was a fourth broadcast, then the screen went blank. Beck typed in a program. The screen flipped and went blank. All other current messages on the shortwave band were normal broadcasts from known sources.

Beck shook his head. "Weird. Real weird."

He stuck his head into the front of the helicopter. Bishop looked sideways at him.

"We rendezvous with the colonel in a couple of minutes." He pointed down where the ocean met the coast with the curving silver line of beaches. "Punta de Amapala. Down there somewhere. What's going on with the radio?"

"Someone with code connections to the Costa Rican base camp we wiped out is broadcasting location coordinates back to a home base. There are four coordinates, and the fourth position is responding twice. Whoever it is, is on the move down there in a big way. I'm going to plot the coordinates I got and raise the colonel."

Bishop looked down over the dark landmass now under them. At a point several miles ahead, a flare suddenly rocketed into the sky just above the tree line, flashing an eerie red glow over the forested terrain.

"Geez," said Bishop. "What the hell was that?"

11

Barrabas gripped his rifle. His eyes scanned the hard faces in the circle of guerrillas. If he was going down, he'd go down firing. Around him, of a single mind, the threatened mercs did the same.

The guerrilla leader stood, feet apart, the light from the dying flare flickering madly across her face and dissolving against the sweat-soaked fatigues that clung wetly to the curves of her body. Her face was framed by jet-black hair that fell carelessly over her shoulders. Her shirt, stretched back by the weight of the cartridge belt she wore, revealed a forceful cleavage. She was the kind of woman men would die for. In different circumstances.

The two armies faced each other in a standoff, tense, silent and watching. No one dared move.

Barrabas felt Lee Hatton's presence beside him and heard her voice low in his ear.

"Colonel, let me deal with this. I've got an inside track."

Barrabas replied without turning his head.

"Go for it, Lee. But if any of them makes a quick move, we open up."

Lee Hatton held her rifle out to her side and stepped forward.

"Rosaria. We have a message. From someone you know," Lee said in Spanish, then named someone. "We have come to destroy Jeremiah."

The guerrilla leader answered without moving. "How do you know him? Who are you?"

Lee handed her rifle to Barrabas and walked closer to Rosaria.

"We must talk."

Rosaria hesitated.

The two women stared hard at each other. Then visibly Rosaria relaxed, her left hand falling from her M-16. She shouted orders out of the side of her mouth to the guerrilla soldiers behind her. Then she turned back to Lee.

"We talk." She slung her rifle over her shoulder. Around her the soldiers lowered their rifles. Barrabas and the SOBs remained frozen.

"They keep their rifles," Lee said, motioning toward the SOBs with a quick sideways jerk of her head.

Again Rosaria hesitated, considering her answer. Finally she said, "They keep their rifles."

Lee walked toward Barrabas and took her rifle back.

"What the hell was that all about?" the colonel asked.

"You said you might need my skills as a diplomat. I'll explain later, okay?" Lee shot him a quick smile and turned back to the waiting Rosaria.

The radio pack beside Billy Two began to beep. He looked at Barrabas.

"It's Nate and Bishop. They're right on time."

Barrabas turned to the guerrilla leader.

"Rosaria, if we don't answer this, there will be trouble for all of us. Our helicopter support."

Rosaria called into the circle of guerrillas standing behind her.

"Manuelo."

A young man barely out of his teens stepped forward.

Rosaria turned back to Barrabas. "Manuelo speaks excellent English. Do not try to mount a counterambush." Then she turned to Lee. "Come." The women strode from the clearing toward the perimeter of the landing zone.

The mercs relaxed slightly into the armed truce between them and the guerrillas.

"It don't make much difference what the circumstances, I don't understand women either way," said Billy Two, bending down over the radio and adjusting the scrambler.

"Can't be too serious anymore if they left us with our weapons," said O'Toole, still eyeing the guerrillas around the clearing with suspicion.

Nanos wiped the tension and sweat from his face with the back of his hand. "That girl is some piece," he said.

"Piece of what, Nanos?" Claude Hayes challenged. "And from the equipment, I'd say she was more woman than girl."

"Can it," Barrabas ordered. There were times when the joking around released the tension. There were other times when it just got on everyone's nerves. This was the other time.

Billy Two was listening intently on the earphones and jotting down the information Beck gave him from the helicopter. In a minute he was tracking the coordinates on a map. The young guerrilla, Manuelo, listened attentively.

"That man is busy," said Barrabas. He looked at the coordinates pinpointed in a wide square on the map of Honduras, trying to figure out what the hell was going on. Then he saw it. Smack dab in the center of everything was the New Society settlement. It was all he needed to confirm what he and Walker Jessup had suspected from the beginning.

"Jeremiah's moving an army," Barrabas said, focusing his concentration on the map. "But at what?"

"We will show you, Colonel Nile Barrabas." It was Rosaria.

She was standing behind him. The stern and beautiful

face was relieved by eyes that now appeared friendly. Lee Hatton stood beside her. Barrabas looked at her.

"Do you want to fill me in now?" he said.

"Jessup. He knows a few people on the political wing of the Liberation Front. Behind the scenes. He briefed me in case we ran into the guerrilla army."

Barrabas shook his head.

"The Fixer fixes it again."

Lee nodded. They both knew that when it came to deals, Walker Jessup could spin circles around anyone, and the circles usually turned out to be a spiderweb. And then it was too late.

"It seems we have the same enemy, Colonel Barrabas." Rosaria placed her finger on the New Society settlement on the map. "This man, Jeremiah, you are right—he is moving his army. We have had our people watch him for a long time now, and our information is good. We know he has been creating an army, and we know he has supplied himself with enough rifles for five hundred men. We did not know what for. But we came here to stop it. To stop this." She motioned toward the bodies lying in the clearing and the still smoldering debris of the helicopter.

"This man is very dangerous," she continued. "He drugs his people through the water they drink. He has a strange power over them so they obey everything he tells them to. We knew about his army, but we did not think they would march for some time yet. They are not well trained. But they have a new kind of rifle that is very dangerous. And we could do nothing. Because for us to cross into Honduras, where the American Army plays war games with the Honduran army, that would be seen as an act of war. And the Americans look for any excuse."

"So where's he going?" Barrabas asked. "Four armies in four different directions? What's his strategy?"

Rosaria looked at the map again. Then she pointed, moving her finger from left to right.

"These are all army positions. The guerrilla army of El Salvador, our comrades, are here. The Salvadoran government is here." She pointed to a third spot. "That is the base built by the Americans for the Honduran army. They supply arms to the *contras*, here, at this base, to fight against Nicaragua. And the Sandinista army of Nicaragua has a border post here to fight against these *contras*."

Barrabas saw it immediately. Three of the four coordinates Beck had picked up led straight to the Salvadoran army, the guerrilla base, and to the Honduran army base. The fourth coordinate led across Honduras along a secondary road. It forked, going toward the *contra* base camp in one direction and toward the Nicaraguan border town in the other.

"He's attacking everyone at once," said Barrabas. "Makes sense in a weird kind of way. They all think they're being attacked by their enemy. So everyone goes to war. And after the holocaust this guy Jeremiah steps in to pick up all the loose pieces. If someone else doesn't beat him to the pieces. Like the Russians."

"Or the Americans," Rosaria added, her voice hard again.

Barrabas turned to Billy Two. "Billy, bring in Bishop and Beck right away."

"So how are we going to stop five hundred soldiers marching in four directions at once?" O'Toole asked, leaning over the map.

"With our help." Rosaria's voice was firm. She clunked the butt of her rifle hard on the ground to emphasize her words. "We know the jungle and the mountains. You do not. But you can fly helicopters. We cannot. Separately we are both nothing. Together we can stop them."

Barrabas nodded his head slowly.

"Can you believe that, Colonel?" O'Toole said. "Americans fighting side by side with Communist guerrillas?" The Irishman shook his head in amazement.

Barrabas looked around him. The carnage. The destroyed helicopter. Lopez. Jeremiah's evil was all around them.

Nanos, Billy Two and Hayes were setting out low-burning flares to mark a landing zone for Bishop. Past the perimeter of lights, the grimy, sweat-streaked faces of Rosaria's guerrilla army waited for orders. They were fighters, warriors, all of them together. SOBs or guerrillas, it didn't matter. They had to put aside their differences to destroy a greater evil. It was that simple.

Jessup and the boys in D.C. didn't know about that kind of thing. They sat at desks and pushed buttons as if they thought they were gods in heaven. Not men living on earth. An earth that would be made hell if men like Jeremiah were left alive.

Barrabas remembered what Jessup had said to him about eliminating Rosaria. Now he knew the Fixer had been set up for it. But that was one of Jessup's problems. The boys in Washington didn't know shit, and sometimes Jessup went along with them.

He looked at Rosaria. "How many soldiers do you have, Rosaria?"

"Twenty-five here. But we can alert our comrades at the base camp to destroy the people headed toward them. It would be dangerous for us to leave El Salvador."

Barrabas pointed to the map. "So we can transport the twenty-five men you have here to stop this group heading toward the El Salvador army positions in Morazán. How do you feel about sending your soldiers to save your enemy's skin?"

Rosaria shrugged. "It is necessary. We must destroy this Jeremiah who thinks he is a god."

"Two down. O'Toole. You, Lee, Bishop and Nate will take this group heading toward the Honduran army base in our helicopter. Hayes has some helicopter experience. He can take that old transport there, drop off the guerrillas near the border, then take Nanos, Billy, and me to stop this group headed toward Nicaragua. After you finish with them, pick us up. Then we go for Jeremiah. Brief them, O'Toole." The big Irishman walked toward the other SOBs.

On the far side of the landing zone, the BK-117 was hovering over the tops of the trees in preparation for a descent. Nanos stood in the circle of flares waving Bishop down.

Rosaria turned to Barrabas.

"And I will go, too. And Manuelo. Both of us know the camp where this Jeremiah is."

Barrabas shook his head. "My gut reaction is—"

"Wrong, Colonel. Is it because I am a guerrilla? Or because I am a woman? You will need us to guide you."

He looked at her, and she stared resolutely back at him, eye to eye. He had faced this once already with Lee Hatton a long time ago, and since then he'd seen her prove herself in battle. Lee and Rosaria were both beautiful women. Dreamgirls, if they wanted to be. They could make any man happy. They could have their choice. And they'd made their choice. They were amazons, making a stand for who they were and what they wanted for their lives.

Barrabas nodded. "All right, Rosaria. But is this the only reason? To guide us?"

"No. I also want a chance to kill this man." Rosaria began walking toward her soldiers. Then she turned back to face Barrabas.

"I would say this man was a devil, but Communists

do not believe in devils. We do not believe in God, either,'' she added.

''What do you believe in, Rosaria?''

''In fighting. For the rights of our people. For justice. And you? Why do you fight, Colonel Barrabas?''

Barrabas smiled. ''I'm what you people call a capitalist. I fight for whoever pays.''

''That is why we have a truce, Colonel Barrabas, and not a peace.'' Rosaria turned. Barrabas pulled out a cigar, bit off the end and spat it out. He watched her walk away.

12

Hayes pulled on the collective and adjusted the rotor. It had been a long time since he'd flown a bird this size. And filled to capacity it was sluggish answering to his adjustments. That didn't matter. It wouldn't be needed much longer.

The green panel lights showed the lines of Barrabas's face in a mask of hard determination.

He didn't like the idea of mass extermination. But Jeremiah's armies had to be eliminated. Eight mercenaries and a couple of dozen guerrillas were hardly enough to wipe out five hundred of the enemy. They'd be slaughtered or exhausted before they finished. Which amounted to the same thing. Dead.

But they had a couple of things on their side. The element of surprise. And a few tricks.

If they pulled it all off with the right timing.

Rosaria leaned forward into the cockpit and pointed to lights glowing up from the distant jungle.

"We are flying along the border now. That is the Honduran army base. The airstrip was built during the war games by your government. There will be American soldiers there, too. We can go down on the highway."

With the light from the stars, Barrabas could just make out a thin straight line below. They fell into silence again as Hayes pushed the heavy bird forward, then dropped altitude.

Rosaria turned back into the fuselage and began giving last orders to the guerrillas who sat against the steel walls.

Hayes brought the helicopter down to a low hover over a deserted stretch of the highway. The guerrillas jumped, running through the howling updraft to the forest. Before Hayes had taken the bird up again, they had already disappeared.

In a few minutes their ambush would be in position. And the army Jeremiah had sent against the Salvadoran army positions would be stopped in its tracks.

In the fuselage, Nanos, Billy Two and Rosaria squatted on the floor staring ahead and waiting for the next stop. Barrabas watched Hayes take the ancient transport back up to cruise altitude and skim it across a landscape potholed with the craters of sleeping volcanoes. Their objective was to stop the army marching against the Nicaraguan government forces and the *contras*. Five of them against two hundred. Not exactly great odds.

Rosaria broke the silence again.

"So now we go to save the CIA-supported *contras* from Jeremiah. Never have I thought I would work so hard to save my enemies from their deaths."

Barrabas said nothing. They were also going to save Sandinistas from attack. It was the first time he'd ever found himself out to save a bunch of Communists. Let alone fight beside them.

BISHOP LANDED THE HELICOPTER facing uphill on the incline above the highway. They followed Manuelo down a thin mountain trail to the ambush zone. The incline continued alongside the highway until it disappeared through a ravine.

The other side of the highway was a hundred-foot drop to nowhere. They took up ambush positions on the hill and waited for the enemy. The only thing in their favor was the geography.

Soon a Land Rover followed by two long buses emerged from the ravine and wound along the highway by the edge of the precipice. Nate Beck followed the convoy with his binoculars. He glanced at his watch. Two and a half minutes.

He heard footsteps coming down the hill behind him. It was Lee.

"All set?" Her voice was calm and reassuring.

"They'll be in the killzone in two minutes."

Lee looked out to where the highway curved out of sight into the ravine. From their vantage point fifty feet up the side of the hill, she could see the dark shapes of the vehicles moving along the road without lights. Farther along the hillside toward the convoy, O'Toole and Manuelo stood by with a MAG. Bishop waited an equal distance in the other direction.

"This is the part of war I've never been too good at," said Beck. "I mean, give me a computer, or the inside of a missile to wire up, and it's made. But this I've never done a lot of."

"Nanos said your aim's very good now," said Lee.

Beck gave a small laugh. The first time he'd fired a rifle grenade, with Alex Nanos lying beside him in the Iranian desert, he was fifty yards off target.

"Yeah, it's better. But deep down inside I'm still a nice Jewish boy from Queens. Know what I mean?"

Lee Hatton nodded. He was talking about killing. "It isn't easy for any of us. After a while you get better at it. But you never get used to it."

She placed a metal box in front of her. A row of wires ran from the bottom of it. The wires were connected to claymores, and the claymores were connected to death in the form of seven hundred densely packed metal balls. When they blew they were fatal to two hundred feet.

With her other hand she pulled back the bolt on her Armalite.

A minute to killzone.

Beck gave two rapid tugs to the cord that ran along the ground beside him.

Fifty feet in either direction Bishop and O'Toole felt the cord tug twice. A minute left. They cocked their rifles. The antipersonnel fragmentation grenades at the end of each barrel loomed over the view of the convoy.

Bishop put his eyes to the nightscope on his rifle. He could see the vehicles moving into the killing ground. He drew a bead on the Land Rover.

The rope jerked once.

Bishop pulled the trigger.

At fifty-foot intervals along the hill, Lee and O'Toole did the same thing.

The Land Rover and both buses took direct hits.

The Land Rover veered out of control and headed for the precipice. It went over. The jangling crash of metal and glass smashing into the rock walls bounced back up from the side of the canyon as it disappeared over the edge.

The first bus careered wildly along the road as the driver died. Lee had scored a direct hit through the front window. It slammed into the hillside, blocking the road. The driver of the second bus braked. Even before it stopped, men were jumping from open doors at either end.

Bishop could already hear the *rat-a-tat-tat* of autofire from positions farther down the hill. It was Manuelo opening up with the MAG and cutting off the rear exit. Bishop slammed another antipersonnel grenade onto his M-16 and aimed for the windows in the middle of the first bus. There were about fifty enemy soldiers in each bus scrambling to get out. The buses were traps. Death traps. Bishop fired.

Liam O'Toole took his cue when the Land Rover took a direct hit. His grenade sailed into the back end of the second bus at the same time that Lee Hatton hit pay dirt on the first one.

They stopped the vehicles. Now they had to stop the enemy.

Soldiers were jumping from the smoking buses and fumbling for their rifles. Others tried to claw their way out of windows, or fell out of doors rolling and shrieking in shrapneled agony.

Beck shot a flare over the tops of the buses. The night lit up over the horror with an unholy glare. Tall shadows of panicking soldiers stretched and danced along the road. The dance of death.

Manuelo sent rounds of bullets down the hill. The first line of soldiers running toward the slope stopped dead in their tracks. They were dead.

The second wave saw their comrades fall. They turned back toward the buses just as the second wave of grenades hit.

Manuelo kept the withering machine-gun fire eating at the road, cutting off retreat. The stream of orange tracers cut up the night, and the barrel reddened with heat. O'Toole dropped his M-16, whipped off the barrel and screwed another one on. Manuelo started firing again. O'Toole grabbed his rifle and started down the hill.

Beck and Bishop worked the Armalites now, firing down the hillside. Cut off from escape in two directions, soldiers ran up the highway.

Lee Hatton pressed a button. The claymores blew. Enemy soldiers lost their legs as they ran, collapsing in tatters of shredded flesh. Bishop followed up with autofire.

For those who still lived, there was only one way out. Straight for the cliff. Their unbroken screams followed them as they plunged to their deaths in the chasm below.

Nate Beck fired another flare to signal Lee and Manuelo to stop their death barrage.

Bishop ran in a crouching zigzag down the hill to his left, and O'Toole came from the other direction until they entered the highway killzone from opposite ends.

The buses were smoking. It sounded as if the highway were moaning.

It was the sound of dying men. The asphalt, torn up where the claymores had blown, was littered with pieces of meat and parts of bodies, twitching limbs attached to shapeless lumps. Out of the gore came the wrenching screams of men still kicking. Their screams grew weaker.

There were enemy soldiers hiding behind the buses.

They didn't have a chance.

Bishop flattened himself on the road and shot under the bus in front of him. Bodies bowled over backward. O'Toole opened up on the other side. Some of the men tried to escape through the space between the two buses. They ran into Lee Hatton, firing from the hill. There was only one way out. Last exit. Over the edge.

Some of them turned and ran, diving off into air and dropping, their screams plunging into the darkness after them.

Others, squeezed between two deaths, turned to fire back at their attackers.

Bishop pulled an empty mag out of his M-16 and jammed another one in. He rolled across the ground as bullets hit close and tar dust exploded on the road nearby. His eyes stung. He rolled five feet and aimed with his eyes closed. He sent new rounds spinning into the night. He rolled again and kept firing. He fired until his mag was empty, rolling and firing, tears streaming from his burning eyes. He rolled, opened them against burning pain and reached for a new mag.

The firing had stopped.

He heard O'Toole's voice. It was calling him.

He jammed the mag in, then wiped his eyes. The tears were washing out the dirt. With his bleary vision he could barely make out the highway. Nothing moved on it.

"Hey, Bishop! Battle's over!" It was O'Toole. Bishop picked himself up.

He felt wet. He looked down at his body. He was covered with blood from head to foot. His fatigues were drenched with it. He was wounded. But it didn't hurt. He patted his body, checking for holes. There were none. Then he saw where the blood came from.

A river of it flowed across the convex surface of the highway onto the shoulders. The killzone. There was nothing human left.

He'd forgotten what it was like.

"Bishop, you okay? Geez, look at this mess." It was Beck.

"Yeah." Bishop shook his head to clear it.

Lee Hatton stood ten feet away, watching.

"Well, I'm relieved," she said. She ran her eyes up and down his body. "For a minute I thought I'd have to sew you up. And from the looks of you it would have taken days."

Shouts echoed down from the hill. The mercs turned and saw Manuelo breathlessly descending the hill.

"Soldiers!" he cried. "Honduran soldiers! They are coming through there!" Manuelo pointed up the highway to the ravine where the enemy soldiers had come from. "They must have heard the noise!"

"Pack it up! Let's move!" O'Toole ordered. Already the headlights from army vehicles were splashing up the highway through the opening of the ravine.

They ran for the helicopter.

BILLY TWO, NANOS AND ROSARIA jumped to the road while Hayes held the ancient transport in a low hover.

"This is it," Barrabas said, turning back to Hayes. "You know what to do. Good luck."

"Just keep me covered, sir. That's all the luck I need." Hayes's brown face blended into the darkness, but his grin shone. He grinned to himself.

He was flying a bomb.

Barrabas jumped. The helicopter moved rapidly away, the rhythmic thud of its rotor fading into the distance.

They stood on a gravel road that curved around the lower slopes of the Cordillera Isabelia near the Nicaraguan border. Two miles away, on one side of the mountain, Jeremiah's convoy headed toward them. Two miles in the other direction, the road forked. One way led to the *contra* encampment. The other went straight into Communist Nicaragua.

Barrabas looked around once to survey the scene.

"Billy, gunner post over there. Nanos, take the HK on the other side. I want the highway covered by fanning action."

The guerrilla force had supplied the American-made M-60 and an old German HK-21. The two machine guns would spit bullets a half mile in broad circular swaths. Where the two arches met, there would be a dip in the range. That would let Barrabas and Rosaria get up close when the time was right.

"Get them out of the vehicles first. Then shoot," said Barrabas as the soldiers went for their positions. Rosaria and Barrabas climbed the hill in long steps. It gave them a great vantage point over the convoy, but no cover except some bushes. Bushes were cover, but they didn't stop bullets. They would have to rely on the night and their own evasive movements.

"Give me your rifle." Barrabas glanced quickly at the serial number as he screwed on an adapter. "Vietnam stock," he said, flicking his eyes up at Rosaria.

She gave a small, womanly laugh. "So many were left behind. And how they travel!"

Barrabas jammed a mag of ballistic bullets into the breech. Then he threw it back to her and handed her two grenades.

"Thermite. Chemical death. Burns through flesh, bone and metal at two thousand degrees centigrade. Go for the ass-end of the trucks and it'll burn through into the fuel tanks."

They separated, taking up positions at the far ends of the killzone. Each man—and one woman—alone and waiting in the dark.

Long training in the military schools of the United States and years as a professional soldier made this kind of maneuver automatic for Nile Barrabas. He waited without noise, his breathing slowing until it seemed he wasn't breathing at all. He was as silent as darkness, as sharp as the night. He became one with the hillside, with the wind, with the rifle he held cocked and ready in his hand. His eyes held the road and the Honduran hills; he searched the air for smells. He was a nerve, wound up, coiled, ready to spring.

He listened.

The sounds of engines straining. Heavy vehicles pulling up a hill.

He watched.

They came into sight, a sharper dark against the night.

He felt the rumble of the trucks through the ground below him, knew the hands on the steering wheel, the feet pushing the pedals as the trucks moved forward.

His eyes moved forward. The barrel of his M-16. The tip of the thermite grenade.

The moment before battle is short. It was in this moment that Barrabas felt true peace. A calm came over him where thought ended and instinct began. When his life was pure action. He was alive. He lived only to deal death. And death would be dealt.

He counted the nine trucks that followed the first. Each truck would have twenty men under the tarpaulin covers. Maybe equipment. Didn't matter. They'd all die.

The parade moved into the killzone.

The first truck was in front of him.

His finger squeezed the trigger.

The grenade whistled with delight.

Boom!

Fourth of July.

Seven hundred and fifty grams of thermite in a steel head knocked on the truck's front door.

Hell's door.

A grenade doesn't wait for answers.

It exploded. The cab was showered with chemical death. It burned through armored metal, then it burned through flesh, muscle and bone. As it burned it produced its own oxygen and burned more.

The burning would last for forty seconds.

An eternity until merciful death.

The truck careened, and a shriek of agony poured from the shattered windshield. The driver braked in his panic and pain. The truck skidded, tipped up and teetered on two wheels.

Then it slammed over sideways onto the road.

It gave Barrabas a great view. A view of the fuel tanks. His rifle was already tipped with the second grenade.

Two hundred yards to his left he heard an explosion. Rosaria scored a direct hit. The engine of the last truck in the convoy blew open. The line of trucks was braking. Men with rifles hopped from the backs onto the road.

Barrabas fired again. The grenade scored. The back

of the fallen truck blew as gallons of gasoline danced in thick oily flames. The soldiers in the back died almost instantly. Their screams were brief.

Rosaria's second incendiary hit. Screams rose up in the darkness until the night overflowed with the agony of death.

Soldiers slit the canvas covers and poured out of the remaining trucks.

Billy Two and Nanos waited.

The soldiers began pouring autofire up the hill at their unseen attackers.

Barrabas slammed the ballistic mag out of his M-16 and pushed in the 5.62s.

The highway was filling up with panicked and excited soldiers. Some were yelling orders. No one listened.

Then Nanos and Billy Two opened up with the HK-21. The ones that didn't die ran for the protection of the trucks. They were fighting back now, firing blindly at their attackers on the hill. Bullets sprayed the ground in front of Barrabas. The rounds were coming fast. Very fast. Faster than he'd ever seen them come before. That was the G-11 at two thousand rounds a minute. A very dangerous rifle.

Barrabas ran back along the hill to a new position. But evasive action was limited against a weapon like that. Then he felt something else. A vibration in the air. He could smell it. It was the helicopter.

HAYES TOOK THE HELICOPTER once around the mountain. Then he swung back toward the road. The action had started. Lights burned up from the highway. Wild lights. Fire.

Hayes put the creaky old bird into descent.

He came down at a run twenty feet above the ground about a half mile off, pushed the throttle, adjusted the rotor and drove it like a hovercraft up the road.

The lead truck had fallen across the road on its side. Hayes swung around it and came back in on an angle. He slowed.

Then they started firing at him.

The bubble blew away on the right-hand side. Hayes jerked on the cyclic control between his legs to swerve back and forth. He brought it down lower. He was running ten feet off the ground now. Bullets ripped into the metal hulk on the right side.

He saw the line of trucks stopped on the road and aimed for the center of them.

He slid back the door and wedged the collective with a crowbar. Then he pounded on a remote charge box on the seat beside him and bailed out.

He hit the road hard but with both feet down and went into a roll. Above him on the hillside, Barrabas and Rosaria supplied covering fire.

The helicopter skimmed along the roofs of the trucks.

Then it exploded. Right on time.

The charges blew in sequence, starting in the nose and working their way back to the tail.

Still hovering in its mad course, it disintegrated into a drifting fireball.

When the fuel tank blew, flames scattered in all directions.

The ancient engines, perched high on the fuselage, flew into the air. Then everything came back down again.

Onto the heads of the enemy below.

Hayes rolled off to the side of the road, a wave of heat sweeping over him from the conflagration.

Then he felt an arm lifting him and pushing him up the hill. Barrabas. They ran higher, away from the heat. Hayes could feel autofire zinging down over their heads.

It was Rosaria giving them cover.

The brave woman stood, legs apart, firing her M-16 relentlessly down the hill.

Hayes and Barrabas stopped and turned to look at what lit up the night behind them.

The men on the road were transformed into running torches. The ones still in the trucks jumped and ran. But the flames followed. Their clothes were on fire.

Then one of the flaming soldiers blew up, bits of his fiery body scattering far and wide. More running men caught fire from the burning debris. Another man blew up. The G-11 caseless cartridges. Something NATO didn't think about. Each man became his own high-explosive incendiary bomb, trapped by the belt of ammunition around his waist.

Shrieks filled the air as men rolled and fell, everyone in his panic trying a different way out.

There was no way out.

The trucks started blowing as the flames spread to the gas tanks.

Highway holocaust.

Honduran hell.

"Let's open up and give the poor buggers a break," said Barrabas.

They blew off their mags into the death below, knocking off the flaming figures, the bodies falling onto the highway and burning. The autofire thinned out as the screams from the human bonfires died.

It was over.

The road was dotted with bodies and bits of bodies.

The flames were greedy, sending an eerie deathlight against the dirty, sweaty faces of the mercs. The putrid, sweet odor of burning flesh mingled with the rank smell of scorched rubber.

The night burned orange.

Nanos and Billy Two appeared silently beside Barrabas, Hayes and Rosaria. They watched the dying flames, momentarily hypnotized.

Barrabas could hear a helicopter approaching. Bishop.

"Let's get the hell out of here," he snapped.

He took the lead, running toward the rendezvous site. The job wasn't finished yet. There was more death to deal.

This time they were going to knock on Jeremiah's door.

And Jeremiah had a lot to answer for.

13

Walker Jessup slammed into a garbage can as he strode along the dirty sidewalk in Panama City. It clattered into the gutter. Half the streetlights were knocked out, and it was hard to see at midnight. Jessup didn't stop. Eyes ahead, searching the facades of buildings, he finally saw what he was looking for. His pace increased until he arrived at the door. He caught his breath and mopped his forehead with a handkerchief.

The neon sign hummed and sputtered as it flashed on and off. The Starlight Lounge. He shoved the handkerchief into his trouser pocket and pushed on the narrow black door. It swung inward. Jessup followed.

The floor was dirty, the walls a grimy yellow. A jukebox played an old fox-trot called "Dancing Cheek to Cheek," and a dozen or so men and women were doing exactly that. The women wore frilly dresses that did nothing to hide their loose flesh, and the heavy layers of makeup hardly concealed the fact that these were over-the-hill whores.

"Over here, soldier. Over here." A tableful of similar creatures stretched out long thin arms for him. Sure they were women who worked hard for a living, but a tableful of them was like a run-in with a giant octopus. Jessup breezed his large figure through the waving tentacles. The man he was looking for was sitting at the bar. Silver John.

The old soldier saw the Texan coming.

"Whooee! If it isn't the Fixer himself! Seems like I

got a lot of company these days. What brings you down this way, Jessup? Wouldn't have anything to do with a couple of other visitors I've had of late, would it?''

Despite the cordial greeting, the old man seemed cool. He waved his hand at a young Panamanian man behind the bar.

''Frankie, hand over that bottle of Johnny Red and a tall glass for the gentleman.''

Jessup got right to the point.

''You saw Barrabas?''

''Might have. But you oughtta know. You got your hand in on most affairs going on in this neck of the woods. What do you want with Barrabas?''

''He's working for me. And a Washington connection to the job turned out to be very bad. So I got a serious problem.''

''Don't have to tell me about Washington. I had lots of experience there before I....'' Silver John looked around at the clientele of the Starlight Lounge. Then he winked at Jessup. ''Till I bought this place. My hideout, Jessup. Seems everyone still manages to find me, though. Haven't seen you since the time we arranged for the replacement of a couple of Southeast Asian presidents. Long time ago. Put on a bit of weight since then, Jessup.''

Silver John slapped the belly that protruded over the belt of Jessup's suit pants. His departure to Panama City had been hurried, and he wore the same suit he had worn on Capitol Hill that afternoon. It was crumpled, sweaty, and the jacket was spotted with the Bloody Mary he spilled down the front of it at a Georgetown cocktail party. A man had sidled up to him and whispered something in his ear. The same man he'd met two days earlier at the Empire State Building in New York.

The information this time was devastating. It shocked Jessup so much he was left standing there holding his glass sideways with tomato juice dripping down his lapels. He wiped himself off with a napkin and made generous goodbyes to his hostess, then grabbed a flight to JFK and another one to Panama City. Six hours later he was in the Starlight Lounge. He hadn't even thought about sponging off the stain on the plane ride. He'd been too busy thinking.

What Barrabas had said to him a few days ago. Barrabas was right. He'd been behind a desk too long. And he'd sold his loyalty, pushed too many buttons and sometimes forgot what was written on those buttons. Life and Death.

The job gave him a lot of power and it made him rich. He'd always been attracted to the good things in life. The easy things. Soft things.

Now *he* was soft. Life was easy. And he'd forgotten what it was like out there in the trenches. Life or death.

And now it looked as if Barrabas was in big trouble on that score. Jessup the Fixer had fixed it good. He helped set up Barrabas for a suicide mission for someone who wanted him out of the way, and suddenly in the middle of a Georgetown cocktail party with a Bloody Mary dripping down his jacket, Jessup realized he had a choice. It was simple. He chose Barrabas. His loyalty wasn't for sale anymore.

A glass of Scotch was shoved into his hand. He swallowed a mouthful. It seemed to give clarity to his thoughts. He put the glass down. A second mouthful would be only the illusion of clarity.

"So what do you want, Jessup? I'm no fool to think you dropped in to say hello. And it better be good, because generally speaking I'm not interested in just anything."

"I got a problem with a certain senator in Washington," Jessup said. Silver John listened carefully, his blue eyes sharp. Jessup continued.

"Seems this senator has had a lot of support of the financial kind from a man named Jeremiah. And in exchange, this senator's done a few favors for this man. Government grants. Testimonials."

"Jeremiah," Silver John mused. "That wouldn't be this tinhorn dictator who runs a settlement up in Honduras?"

Jessup nodded.

"Heard about him. Don't like what I heard. This got something to do with young Nile?"

Jessup nodded again. "We've been having a few problems in Central America. We sent in Nile to eliminate the source of these problems. At the time, we weren't sure if it was Jeremiah or not."

"Now you're sure."

Jessup nodded again.

"And who's this 'we' you're talking about?"

"Not important. But high."

"Higher than the senator?"

"Much higher. But the senator's been in the way."

"Get to the point, Jessup."

"This senator was involved in the decision to send Barrabas and the SOBs into Central America. At the same time, he was making a fact-finding tour of El Salvador, touring irrigation projects, stuff like that. But tonight I got word. He's making an unannounced stop. At the New Society settlement. To see Jeremiah. To warn him about Barrabas." Jessup looked at his watch. "In seven hours."

Silver John wasn't looking at Jessup anymore. He stared at his hands on the bar. One of them held a highball glass and the highball glass was full. Silver John pushed the glass away to the far side of the bar. Then he looked at Jessup.

"So what do you want?"

"I need a helicopter and a pilot. Tonight. Now."

"Frankie!" Silver John called to the man behind the bar again. "Telephone."

The young man pulled it out from under the counter and put it in front of Silver John. The old warrior dialed a number and waited. Someone answered. Silver John spoke a few terse sentences of rapid Spanish. Then he hung up and looked at Jessup.

"You got your helicopter. In one hour."

"And a pilot?"

"Pilot was a little harder. But I got you a real good one."

"Someone you've worked with?"

"Well, Jessup, I'll tell you. This bum leg of mine keeps me from getting around. But in my day I was the finest helicopter pilot in the U.S. Marine Corps. So do you wanna get going, or do you just wanna sit here and talk about it?"

Jessup nodded quickly.

"Let's go," was all he said.

BISHOP TURNED the BK-117 as he landed to face it into the wind for takeoff. He came down on the highway a quarter of a mile up the road from the death scene. Hardly had the skids touched the highway than the airman was out of his seat and running toward Barrabas.

"We're going to have some problems loading, Colonel. We didn't allow for two extra people and the equipment, too."

"Are we going to be over maximum weight?"

Bishop shook his head.

"The problem is air density. We've already got high altitude and high temperature. The air's thin. That reduces the permissible load."

"Can we do it?"

"We can," Bishop said slowly. "But what we're gaining in weight we lose in performance. And there's the question of balance—how we distribute the weight so we don't throw off the center of gravity. Otherwise we take the risk of losing the tail rotor or scratching up the windshield on the side of the mountain.''

''Billy, bring the maps here! Rosaria!'' Barrabas shouted. He turned to Bishop again. ''You get them in the helicopter and tell them where to sit. We'll go as far as we can, then bail out and do the rest on foot.''

Billy Two and Rosaria jogged up to Barrabas's side as Bishop went back to the helicopter, directing the mercenaries into the BK-117.

Billy Two already had the map unrolled over his knee.

The swirls of topographical lines over the Honduran countryside looked like fingerprints. They marked the craters of the volcanic ranges that surrounded them.

''He is here.'' Rosaria pointed to one of the craters. ''The Quentoya volcano. There is a valley between it and this other volcano, Pentayan. Here it opens out into farmland. But here, where the river flows between the two volcanoes, that is where the camp is.''

''Have you seen it?'' Barrabas asked.

Rosaria hesitated. ''Once,'' she said. ''The camp is surrounded by a steel fence along the river and up the sides of the mountain. There is a gate at the bottom of the valley, with guards. Here—'' she pointed halfway up Quentoya ''—the fence ends because there are cliffs on both sides that cannot be climbed. Jeremiah's head-quarters is halfway up the side of the volcano between these two cliffs, and looks down over the camp.''

''So there's only one way to Jeremiah other than through the front gate,'' Barrabas said.

''Yes. Over the volcano.'' Again Rosaria leaned to-ward the map. ''We must fly from here, to here.'' Her finger leaped across the lines on the map. ''Almost forty miles. The pilot will know which mountain is Quentoya, because it is the highest along this ridge. We can land there. There is forest on the mountain, but I know where there is a clearing.'' Again the guerrilla leader hesitated. ''A landing zone,'' she said finally. ''Then we must go overland. About ten miles. But when we reach the top, we will look down over Jeremiah.''

''And how many guards will there be at the top of the mountain?''

''None. They think that the mountain is impassable. They are wrong. You will see.''

''All right, let's move it.'' Barrabas stood, and the three of them ran for the helicopter.

Bishop waited for them outside. ''Colonel, if you could take the copilot's seat, Billy in the fuselage right behind me, and Rosaria at the back.''

Barrabas looked through the windshield. Lee Hatton was already sitting in the copilot's seat.

Bishop sounded apologetic.

''Uh, sir, I need lots of weight up front to counterbalance the load in back. You'll have to share the seat. If you don't mind, sir.''

''As long as you get this thing off the ground, Bishop.'' Barrabas climbed in.

''Which is it going to be, Colonel?'' Lee laughed. ''You on my lap or me on yours?''

''Half and half, Hatton.'' He slid into the seat and Lee lifted her body, pulling herself over against the cyclic control between the two front seats. By the time they wedged themselves in, Bishop was in the pilot's seat and had the rotor turning.

With single-minded concentration, he adjusted the controls with smoothness and precision to account for the different center of gravity. Barrabas could feel that the movements were sluggish. Slowly the weighted helicopter rose off the ground into a hover.

''Perfect,'' Bishop muttered to himself, completely absorbed in the delicate maneuvers he made with the controls. He had the BK-117 in a straight-line horizontal hover. His hand reached out to ease forward the cyclic, then he increased the collective with his left hand. Slowly the nose of the helicopter settled forward and rose into a climbing attitude.

They were moving.

Bishop breathed out in relief. "Actually, I wasn't sure if we'd get this thing up or not."

"Bishop, you're doing fine," said Barrabas. "How fast can she move?"

"Not fast. Cruise speed is down to about seventy miles an hour. Just let me know where to take her down."

Bishop followed the silver line of a river below the helicopter as it wound its way through the valley of the volcanoes. The land below was pockmarked with craters. With night spread across the land, they felt as if they were flying over the dark side of the moon.

Half an hour later they saw the Quentoya peak looming up ahead at the end of the long valley. Bishop coasted over the top of the forest until it began to climb up the steep side of the volcano.

The helicopter lurched and bumped in a downdraft. Bishop cursed.

"We're on the leeward side of the mountain, and the air currents are rough. The mountain chops them all up, like water coming over a fall."

The helicopter jumped again, and Bishop pulled it higher, his hands moving along the controls as if it were second nature.

He continued to climb, keeping the BK-117 above the trees as he rose over the slopes of the mountain on a thirty-degree angle from the river.

Then he saw the landing zone.

It was a hundred-foot plateau where the forest line broke along the side of the volcano.

"Ask Rosaria what's down there," Bishop said quickly, his hands still moving on the controls. Again the helicopter bucked in the turbulent airstream.

The question was passed back to Rosaria in the cabin and then back up front. Billy Two leaned around into the front seat.

"She says grass. High grass. But the ground is flat."

Bishop cursed again. It couldn't be worse. Grass absorbed the air cushion, which made it harder to hover, and he had enough problems as it was. He increased the manifold pressure.

Slowly the helicopter lowered into a hover as it descended below tree level into the clearing. The powerful downstream from the rotors flattened the grass in the gray light.

The skids touched earth. The helicopter shuddered and jumped once before settling. Bishop stopped the rotor. They were down.

The mercs jumped from the helicopter into the clearing, forming a line as they did and passing equipment, rifles and ammunition along to one another out of the belly of the aircraft, making a pile on one side of the clearing.

Everyone knew what to do. No words were necessary.

Barrabas stood by the helicopter talking to Bishop. Then he called Nate Beck over from the line of mercs passing matériel from the helicopter fuselage.

"Sir!" Beck jogged up quickly beside the leader.

"I want you to stay here with Bishop. We'll go in over the volcano and hit from the top. But we need a diversion. We'll radio to let you know. Then Bishop's going to fly in over the front gates. You're going to take out the gates. With this."

Barrabas handed him an M-16 with a 40mm grenade launcher on the forestock. Attached to it was an antitank grenade. Barrabas pulled more off his belt and laid them on the floor of the helicopter.

"I dunno, sir. I haven't had great luck with these before. I mean, I'm great with electronics stuff, but—"

"You've been training, haven't you?"

Beck nodded.

"So look." Barrabas showed him the primary quadrant and secondary leaf and post sights on the grenade launcher.

"Use these and you can't miss, Nate. I wouldn't have you do it if I didn't know you could."

"Yes, sir."

Barrabas looked at his watch. The volcano looming up over the clearing was outlined by a thin purplish light. They were on the western side. On the eastern side, where the New Society camp lay, morning was just beginning to break.

It would be almost full daylight by the time they got there.

He turned back to Bishop.

"Do two or three passes along the perimeter of the gate with as much damage as possible. And take care of this bird. I'm counting on you to fly us out of there when it's all over."

He turned toward the other SOBs waiting at the side of the clearing.

"Rosaria and I take point," Barrabas said. "O'Toole."

"Sir!" The big red-haired Irishman appeared at his side.

"Who's got the launchers?"

"Nanos and Billy Two now, sir. And we got the rappelling equipment from the helicopter."

"We quick-march it up the side of the mountain fifteen and walk fifteen. The launchers are too heavy for one to carry all the way, so we'll change packs every half hour."

"Are you ready, Colonel Barrabas?" Rosaria asked.

He nodded. "How long will it take?" he asked.

"Two hours. The trail leads back and forth along the edge of the mountain. I know it well."

"I suppose you use it for smuggling arms into El Salvador from Nicaragua. Is that why you know this country?"

Rosaria was silent. Then she said, "And you, Colonel? Will you turn in complete intelligence reports to your government?"

Barrabas strapped the buckles of his pack around his chest. "Rosaria, if and when we get out of here, I forget everything. Okay?"

The guerrilla nodded. "I didn't think I would ever find myself trusting an American mercenary, Colonel Barrabas. But I will trust you."

She walked quickly toward the end of the clearing where she disappeared into the scrub forest. Barrabas followed, and after him the line of soldiers.

The night was still pitch-black on their side of the volcano, and it was impossible to see where they were going. But Rosaria knew the trail. She jogged forward confidently. The trail stayed clear, the ground firm underfoot.

After an hour they rose above the tree line and rested five minutes to change packs and have water before pushing on.

The sky on the other side of the mountain grew a lighter purple, and the purple seeped into a dark musky blue as the hot tropical sun began its steep climb over the Honduran landscape. Already they could feel the heat of the day beginning. But the sweat that drenched their clothes came from the climb up the mountain.

Slowly, it seemed, the pancake-flat top of the volcanic crater grew larger and closer, until finally as the daylight grew bright enough to give clarity to their surroundings, they found themselves on top of the mountain, the edge of the crater just overhead. Rosaria turned to her right, and the trail began leading down.

For another half hour they turned and snaked their way along the edge of the volcano, doubling back where it became too steep, then pushing forward again. Finally Barrabas could see that fifty feet ahead of them the trail ended at a short plateau and a precipice. Rosaria put up her hand to stop them, then began removing her pack.

"We have arrived," she said.

Barrabas quickly undid the straps of his pack and dropped it on the black volcanic rock. The others did the same.

"Come, I will show you." Rosaria motioned to him.

They approached the edge of the precipice, dropping to the ground and pulling themselves forward with their elbows.

At the precise moment they reached the edge of the cliff, the eastern sun pulled itself above the far horizon. Its beacons of yellow light exploded across the far mountains and into the valley that spread out below.

Far to the east were acres of flat farmland filled with coffee and banana plants. Directly below, the valley narrowed between the volcano they were on and a farther one, exactly as Rosaria had described.

At the bottom of the valley where a river flowed, rows of small buildings like army barracks surrounded a central plaza. Jeremiah's New Society.

The camp was walled in by a high wire fence topped with rolls of razor wire. Through his binoculars Barrabas could see conductors leading from the guardhouse at the main gates. The fence was electrified, as well.

The volcano and the two massive arms of lava rock that stretched out on either side of the camp formed natural defensive walls.

Rosaria pointed to the far cliffs.

"There are trails that lead down from the top into the valley outside the fence."

Barrabas nodded. The tops of the cliffs were perfect for the grenade launchers, too.

There was an eighty-foot drop from the precipice where they lay to the rocks below. Five hundred yards farther down the hill Barrabas could make out the roofs of several buildings along a stream. Jeremiah's compound, where the madman could stand and look out over his little kingdom.

Barrabas could see signs of activity in the early-morning light. Guards patrolled the gate at the main guardhouse, and a group of men bearing rifles stood at the central plaza. He shifted his focus to the narrow streets that ran through the rows of buildings. He could see women leaving some of the houses and moving toward a larger one set near the central plaza.

Two men walked down the long wide steps that led from Jeremiah's compound on the side of the hill to the plaza below. There was no sign of anyone who fitted the giant's description. If they struck soon at the compound on the side of the hill, chances were good that they'd get him there.

"How many soldiers do you figure he has left in there?" Barrabas asked Rosaria.

She shrugged casually. "Perhaps fifty armed men. Not many. And five hundred followers who are not armed."

Outnumbered again.

"The one advantage we have is surprise. And they don't know how many of us there are. We can use the multiple grenade launchers on automatic timers, and they'll think a division is going in after them with air support and artillery backup," said Barrabas.

Then he noticed the glint of sunlight on metal in the

sky over the fields far down the valley in the east. He brought up his binoculars and turned the focus to infinity.

It was very small, but it was unmistakable. It was a helicopter. And it was coming in for a landing. Suddenly there was more activity in the plaza. They were waiting for the helicopter to land.

"Who is it?" Rosaria asked urgently.

He switched his view back up to the helicopter.

"I don't know yet."

It filled his view.

It had a star and stripes painted on the tail.

Then he saw the eagle crest on its door.

What the hell was going on? he wondered.

It was an official government helicopter. Government of the U.S.A.

"Who is it?" asked Rosaria again.

He told her.

"And now, Colonel Barrabas?"

Her tone was doubtful.

"We attack. Immediately! I don't care who the hell's down there. We're gonna clean out this viper's nest once and for all, and we're gonna clean it good."

MORNING BROUGHT SUN, and the sun warmed the Honduran forests, the fields of coffee and the orchards of banana trees. It dried the dampness from the leaves into a light mist. Then the mist was lifted from the valley, and daylight became piercing in its clarity.

The smells of tropical greenery and the sweet perfume of coffee flowers rested on the air. In the bushes outside Jeremiah's house, hummingbirds swarmed around the blossoms of giant flowers and parakeets flitted about the shrubs, squawking their tiny, imperfect songs.

It was paradise.

But not for Jeremiah.

The giant looked out over his valley with his arms

folded across his chest, surveying the first signs of activity. His men had gathered in the plaza below. Far off, in the distant sky, the senator's helicopter approached.

Things were not going well for Jeremiah.

The senator was his last chance.

His armies had marched into the Honduran night six hours ago. And vanished. Radio contact ended. It was as if they'd fallen into some abyss and disappeared from the face of the earth.

Fifteen years of planning and conspiring had evaporated like the mist from the jungle under the morning sun.

The first glorious rays of yellow burst into the room like symphonic music, washing across the brooding giant and striking the small, crumpled shape of Glen Beam clinging to sleep on the gigantic sofa at the back of the enormous room.

He stirred and twisted, pushing the sunlight away. Then he opened his eyes sharply. For a moment, as he saw his surroundings again, they were filled with shock.

As if eyes in the back of his head had seen Beam awaken, Jeremiah turned from the window.

Jeremiah hadn't slept all night.

It showed. His face was long and terrible, and covered with a grisly sheen of sweat.

Beam pushed himself up and swung his feet to the floor.

"Come here," the giant's voice boomed.

Beam raised himself from the sofa and walked to the window.

"There." Jeremiah pointed. Beam followed the direct line of the index finger. At the bottom of the mountain, in the central plaza, a helicopter with the seal of the United States government was landing. A dozen of Jeremiah's black-uniformed men had taken up positions around the landing zone.

"I will still win," Jeremiah said. His voice was flat, suppressing an anger that threatened to explode. An anger that Jeremiah knew he had to control because if he didn't, he would begin to destroy. Things. People. It didn't matter. His bare hands were strong. No one could stop him.

"That's great, man," said Beam, wiping sleep from his eyes and not understanding the drama unfolding before him. "Did you make contact with your armies yet?"

"My armies are no longer necessary. There are many ways to accomplish the same thing."

Beam nodded eagerly. He wanted to keep Jeremiah happy.

"So who's that coming in down there?"

"That is the man who has come here because he thinks he is more powerful than I am. But he will learn, now that he is here, that he is my servant, not my master." Jeremiah named the senator. Beam nodded.

"Very good, Jeremiah. Very, very good."

The helicopter landed in the plaza, and as the rotor slowed, it was ringed by armed men. A short man stepped out, followed by two men in suits and a shapely blond woman. Black-uniformed guards rushed forward and grabbed them. Beam could see the short man having a fit. A guard threw him at two other men who grabbed his arms and walked him up the slope of the mountain toward Jeremiah's house. The other three passengers stood with their hands in the air.

Beam turned from the window. His own helicopter was still parked at the far side of the central plaza. He wanted to go, but he didn't know whether he should ask or just try to slip away. Either method might end in failure. And he didn't know if they'd filled the gas tanks of his helicopter. He decided to be straightforward.

"Did you manage to get your people to put some fuel in my helicopter?"

Jeremiah turned and looked at Beam, his dark eyebrows high and curled like horsewhips.

"No." Jeremiah turned back to the window. The senator was now climbing up the steps followed by two armed guards. He looked indignant and scared.

"Jeremiah, I've really gotta get going. I have business—"

"Shut up, fly! Or I will squash you!" the giant shouted with such fury that the room trembled.

Beam walked back to the sofa and sat sulkily. He was trapped.

A guard appeared at the doorway.

Again Jeremiah turned as if he had seen the man's entrance through the back of his head.

"Bring him to me," he said.

The uniformed man disappeared. Beam could hear movement of people entering the house. An American voice was making a lot of noise. The voice sounded offended. Suddenly a short, gray-haired man appeared at the doorway followed by black-uniformed guards.

"I am furious! I have *never* been treated. . .Jeremiah! I demand to know what exactly—"

"Senator." Jeremiah's voice was low and calm. The giant still stood by the window, his arms folded across his chest.

"Jeremiah, you have gone too far!" the senator began. "Do you think I don't know who is behind the killing of these advisors, the smuggling of weapons into Central America? Do you have any idea the lengths I've gone to in Washington to keep this secret?"

Jeremiah listened stiffly as the senator spoke. Then he pointed at the senator with his entire arm and in a low, dangerous voice said, "You will shut up. You will tell me what I want to know. You will tell me now."

The senator tried to look firm, but his eyes filled with fear, and his voice had the thin edge of panic.

"Look, Jeremiah, you've already done enough damage...."

Jeremiah bounded across the room in three long strides and grabbed the senator by the collar of his shirt. His immense hand reached down and folded around the little man's tie, and the long arm of Jeremiah held him high in the air. The senator's cries of protest came out as mere squawks hardly distinguishable from those of the parakeets in the gardens outside the house. His hand clawed wildly at Jeremiah's arms, and his feet and legs dangled in the air.

Jeremiah's voice boomed again, thick with threats of death.

"You will tell me what has happened to my base in Costa Rica, what has happened to the armies who marched out last night, who has been sent against me, how many there are and when they will come here. You will tell me everything, Senator, or I will destroy you like a little bug who annoys me."

Jeremiah pivoted and threw the senator off his hand onto the giant sofa, which caught him like a trampoline, throwing him forward and back before he came to a terrified rest.

The senator told him everything.

14

Barrabas stuck his finger in the center of the diagram scratched in the dirt on the mountain plateau.

"We rendezvous here. Fight our way in to the central plaza. There are two helicopters there. One's the Raven." His sharp blue eyes sought out the faces of the soldiers. They all knew what he was saying. Beam was still in there. And they had Lopez to avenge.

Barrabas went on. "Make sure none of those helicopters leave. Bishop will come in there to take us out." Again he glanced at their faces.

"Lee, Rosaria, Manuelo and I will go down over the edge and straight for the command house." He looked at Lee. Her eyes were steady.

The SOBs lacked the protection of night, so if they had to go in by day to blaze their trail through hell, they would. But no one had any illusions about the danger they faced. And broad daylight wasn't going to help.

"O'Toole, I want you and Hayes over on the western bluffs with the grenade launcher. Nanos and Billy Two, take the eastern bluffs. Take enough grenades for two strikes. Twenty-four each. When you see Bishop come in and take out the front gates, fire the first round. Set up again, put the launchers on the timers, and start down the trails to the valley. As soon as you get to the fence, blow it open and go in."

They jumped to their feet and started to get ready. Billy Two and O'Toole hoisted the launchers onto their backs as Hayes and Nanos counted out ammo. Rosaria pointed out the trails, and the mercs quickly disappeared in the direction of their positions.

Rosaria and Manuelo wrapped the twelve-foot sling ropes for rappelling down the cliff as Lee secured the long rope to a tree on the hillside. Then she inched forward on her stomach with the hundred-foot coil of rope over her back until she was at the edge of the precipice and looking down over the valley.

A few minutes later Barrabas joined her. The sun was resting above the horizon now, the new day bright, and the breeze blowing up the side of the volcano was redolent with the freshness of luxuriant growth in the green valley below.

He peered through the binoculars at the bluffs to the east. Finally he saw Claude Hayes on his belly, moving back from the edge, feeding out a coil of wire to the grenade launcher. On the west side of the volcano, the small deadly darts of a dozen PRB grenades mounted on their spigots showed on the top of the bluffs. Billy Two and Nanos were nowhere to be seen, covering themselves behind an abutment of rock.

They were ready.

Barrabas kept his eyes on the binoculars and looked far down the valley as it narrowed between the rows of volcanic peaks in the west.

He saw it as a tiny white fleck in the sky, sparkling a little sometimes from the sunlight. It grew bigger quickly because it was coming on fast. Bishop was pushing the BK-117 all out at 170 mph straight toward the big front gates.

In the settlement, they noticed.

There was a sudden flurry of activity. Black-garbed soldiers ran from the central square down the half-mile-long avenue toward the main entrance.

Finally the sound of machine-gun fire echoed up from the valley. They were firing from the guard tower at the BK-117 as it came in.

Without slowing its incredible speed, Bishop zig-zagged the white bird madly in the sky while still bearing down on his target.

Bullet chatter became thicker as the helicopter came within range of their automatic rifles. The BK-117 swooped sideways, then zoomed in over the perimeter fence. Still turning the copter on its side, Bishop brought it back in an arc over the gate and straightened out briefly. Long enough for Beck to fire.

Right on, Nate.

The guard tower blew into a column of flame.

The helicopter soared out of range as Bishop arced up. Already he began turning it to take Beck in for a second run at the gates.

From all over the camp, soldiers were running for the main gates. Barrabas put the binoculars down and threw the rappelling line over the edge. It spiraled down eighty feet to the rocks below.

He gave the camp one last look as Billy Two and O'Toole sent the first PRB grenades on their appointed rounds from their opposite positions. Buildings at the edge of the camp on both sides exploded in flames.

Barrabas snapped his rappel link onto the rope and tugged it between his legs. He positioned himself with his right hand in the small of his back to brake with. His left hand held the fixed end of the rope for guidance and balance.

"Meet you down there," he said to Lee and Rosaria. He crow-jumped off the edge, legs parallel to the ground, and slid down the long rope toward Jeremiah's compound.

"TEN MERCENARIES! Five hundred of my soldiers disappear into the night without a word, without a trace, and you tell me you have sent only ten men against me?"

Jeremiah strode quickly back and forth across the

room, wiping his hands continually on the lapels of his white jacket. The sweat on his palms betrayed his nervousness, though his voice did not.

He stopped briefly to watch four of his soldiers quickly descend the steps to the plaza below. He didn't have many armed soldiers left now.

"No way, Jeremiah." Beam was backing the giant up, his voice slippery with deception. "How can ten men wipe out five hundred soldiers? The man's lying."

"I swear, Jeremiah." The senator gulped. He stood in the center of the huge room wringing his hands, his elbows tight against his body, his shoulders hunched as if by closing in on himself he could cut out the fear.

Fear of Jeremiah.

Jeremiah had the look of a killer in his eyes. Even the senator was not too blind to notice.

"If you'll just hold tight, Jeremiah," the senator went on. "Forget all this. Forget about Central America. Just let me use your radio, and I'll do what I can to have the special force called off, I'll...."

The senator prattled on, begging for his life.

Jeremiah turned his back on him and surveyed his endangered kingdom with his arms folded defiantly across his chest.

Then he saw the BK-117 streaming in from the blue heavens to blow out the gates of hell.

Blow.

The guard tower blew into a column of flame, and the helicopter spun around for more.

Jeremiah's eyes grew wide. Finally he lost the control he had worked so hard to keep all night. He lost his temper.

He drew a small radio from his pocket and pressed it on. His voice came out of his throat in a savage whisper.

"Kill them. Now." He clicked the radio off and crushed it in his fist.

On the plaza below, two men immediately opened up with autofire. The senator's aides and the blond secretary fell dead onto the pavement.

Then Jeremiah turned. He looked at the senator and started to move.

Bloodlust. His eyes were empty of all else.

The senator saw it. He froze. His body drew in as if he were trying to make himself invisible.

Glen Beam moved slowly back toward a wall, out of the way.

The senator opened his mouth, but no words came. He was a goner. He had spent a lifetime playing broker in the game of power. It was no good to him now. He had none. He was power broke.

Jeremiah advanced. The senator stumbled back, his face glued to the giant's eyes.

The sounds of explosions outside swelled, punctuated by the *chat-a-chat-chat* of automatic rifles. More explosions and then screams.

Jeremiah's long arm reached out and grabbed the senator by his collar.

The giant roared.

"You puny little thing! You have betrayed me, you spineless *politician*!" He spat the word.

With one hand he raised the terror-stricken senator high in the air by the man's collar. With his other hand he grabbed the crotch of the senator's pants. He held the man sideways with his arms and legs flailing and kicking desperately in midair. The senator shrieked in horror.

Jeremiah raised his left leg.

He cracked the senator's body over his knee as if it were firewood. The senator's spine snapped like a twig.

The man stopped shrieking.

The sounds of explosions and rifle fire poured into the room.

Jeremiah threw the body into a corner, where it landed like a discarded rag doll.

Glen Beam ran for the door.

Fast.

BARRABAS STRAIGHTENED HIS LEGS, clenched his right hand around the rope to brake and hit the ground with knees bent to soften the impact. Before he let go of the rope, he could feel it moving as Rosaria started her descent.

The sounds of battle already floated up from the valley.

He unhooked himself with one hand, while bringing his M-16 around and into the trigger finger of the other. It was one swift movement. He turned and was facing down the slope, ready.

He heard something that sent chills spiraling up his back.

The sounds of explosions and rifle fire were joined by another sound. The beat of a drum. Slowly, almost imperceptibly, another sound rose up from behind the drumbeat. He could barely make it out. Then it grew louder, and he heard the sounds of hundreds of voices chanting ''Je-re-mi-ah, Je-re-mi-ah.''

He looked down into the valley.

The guard tower and a half-dozen buildings around the perimeter of the camp were burning madly. Broad sections of the gate along the front of the fence were blown away, and in the distance he could make out the BK-117 coming in again. Beck's shooting had been deadly. As the remaining soldiers in the settlement rushed to defend their camp, they were caught by the grenades Beck threw from the bird. The ground was peppered with black-uniformed bodies.

At the far sides of the camp, where the perimeter fence

met the stone bluffs of the volcano, more explosions threw smoke and debris into the air as two more SOB attack parties blew their way in.

What remained of Jeremiah's army retreated toward the center of the camp, throwing sporadic gunfire back at their attackers.

Above it all, the chanting swelled to a roar as hundreds of people poured from the buildings of the New Society camp into the central square. They moved into groups and long lines, swarming like ants on honey. The chanting grew louder.

Rosaria landed with a thud beside Barrabas.

"It is terrible, you will see," said the guerrilla leader, unhooking herself and letting the rope free for Manuelo and Lee. "We must stop him now."

Before Barrabas could stop Rosaria she was gone, her M-16 in one hand, the other out to balance herself as she jumped down the rocky slopes toward the roof of Jeremiah's house.

"Rosaria!" he shouted after her. She disappeared into the trees above the edge of the stream.

Manuelo thumped to the ground behind Barrabas.

"Rosaria went off down there. I'm going after her. Wait here for Lee, then follow," Barrabas ordered the young guerrilla soldier.

Then he darted down the rocky slope.

THE GRENADE LAUNCHERS HAD SCORED WELL. By the time Claude Hayes and Liam O'Toole scraped down the narrow trail to the bottom of the volcanic bluffs, people were screaming and running from burning buildings near the fence. The flames leaped high, licking with delight at the wooden structures.

O'Toole pulled a high-explosion grenade from his belt and shoved it into Hayes's hands.

"Let's blow our way in there, Hayes, clean it up, and get the hell out of here. I want a whiskey so bad I can already taste it."

"Last one through the fence buys, Liam." Hayes rammed the grenade onto the rifle launcher.

They aimed together.

They scored together.

A long section of the fence blew apart. The roof of another building caught fire.

As the sound of the explosion died, another sound took over. A steady, rhythmic drumming beat, low at first but quickly becoming louder.

People poured from the houses and ran up the long straight streets toward the center of the camp.

The sounds of the chanting grew louder.

The two mercs heard the name of the man they were going to destroy thrown into the air in an insane exaltation.

Hayes looked at O'Toole and O'Toole looked at Hayes. The look on both their faces said, What the hell is that?

They ran for the hole in the fence and crossed the perimeter into the camp unopposed.

Then six guards came speeding down one of the long streets from the central plaza.

Hayes dived forward onto his stomach, keeping his M-16 high and firing as he hit the ground.

The guards fell back. Three hit the ground, dead. The other three started running back the way they came.

O'Toole shot from the hip. The big Irishman was relentless.

One by one the three fleeing guards went down. The way was clear.

Hayes picked himself up, and they ran past burning, empty houses toward the central plaza.

ON THE OTHER SIDE OF THE CAMP, Alex Nanos and Billy Two ran through the hole they had blown in the fence.

The sound of the steady drumbeat and the chanting of Jeremiah's name was a deafening chorus beating out from the center of the camp, as mysterious to them as it was to O'Toole and Hayes.

The streets along the edge of the camp were deserted. They turned right and ran along the perimeter of the fence to the edge of a row of buildings.

A soldier in the black uniform of Jeremiah's army darted out from around the corner of a house, his automatic rifle firing at Billy Two. The Indian threw himself into a roll along the dusty ground.

Nanos stopped with his M-16 in front of him and gave the man a 3-round burst across the chest. Two out of three hit. Not bad. The guy was dead.

But he had friends.

They came running around the corner of the building firing at the Greek.

But Billy Two had already pulled the pin on the grenade. He threw it.

BAM! Dogmeat.

Nanos threw Billy Two a quick look that said Thanks, pal, and they ran on. And suddenly braked.

What they saw was horror.

Along the edge of the plaza, water gushed from the pipes winding down the hillside from Jeremiah's compound. The water gushed into long troughs at the edge of the plaza.

Jeremiah's people ran for the troughs of water, chanting as they ran, their faces streaming with tears. In a mad panic, they filled their cups with water and drank it as they ran to the other side of the plaza.

Some of them made it; most of them didn't. In midrun they shuddered and stopped, their eyes swelling enormously from their heads, Jeremiah's name grinding out between clenched teeth as a last horrible lungful of air gave way. Dead, the bodies fell stiffly in heaps around the plaza.

And still the living ran on, chanting their leader's name to the horrible drumming from the loudspeakers, filling their cups, drinking and dying on the run. The ground was littered with hundreds of bodies.

At the edge of the plaza stood the major persuasion: black-garbed soldiers firing their rifles at people who balked and tried to run away.

Those who didn't die of the poison died of hot lead.

Billy Two threw a second grenade. It caught a party of soldiers and silenced their action. Farther on, another grenade blew up and more of the soldiers died.

O'Toole and Hayes coming in from the other side.

Then Nanos caught Billy Two by the shoulder and pointed savagely with the barrel of his rifle.

At the center of the plaza.

The U.S. government helicopter stood with its doors open. The bodies of the two aides and the blond secretary lay in pools of blood by the skids.

A thin man with long blond hair was making a run for it. For the helicopter. Glen Beam.

Nanos made a run for it, too.

Billy Two was right behind him, dodging the piles of bodies twitching on the pavement. Jeremiah's people were too busy drinking their cyanide to notice the mercs running through the crowd.

Beam was in the helicopter.

Nanos went down on one knee.

The rotor was turning.

Nanos started firing.

The skids rose off the ground.

Billy Two plucked a grenade from his belt.

The helicopter moved forward.

Billy pulled the pin.

Nanos fingered the trigger. Bullets glanced off the armored sides of the official craft.

He pulled the M-16 down from its recoil and aimed at the pilot's open window.

The helicopter rose higher, Beam frantic at the controls.

The chanting was beginning to fall off, but still men and women drank from their cups and died in horrific pain. Corpses piled higher around the mercs.

Billy Two threw the grenade at the window like a fastball.

The helicopter rose higher.

The grenade hit the door and bounced down.

It blew under the copter, spreading shrapnel into the already dead bodies piled on the ground.

The helicopter was up and away.

Nanos kept firing as if he could blow the helicopter out of the sky by sheer willpower alone. Firing for Lopez.

Beam gave him the finger from the pilot's window, then turned for the open valley to the east.

"Now you die, devil!" Rosaria shouted at Jeremiah from the door of the building.

Jeremiah turned from the water tanks and faced the amazon in all her fierceness. He had released all the cyanide into the water supply. Somehow it made him feel better to know that if he wasn't going to survive, no one else would either. Rosaria raised her chin high and held her M-16 at her waist.

"I have never been more glad to kill someone," she said, "than to kill you for all the people you destroy."

Jeremiah smiled at her. A big, broad smile across his foot-wide face.

She fired a 3-round burst into his chest.

The giant didn't move. He kept smiling. His shirt and

suit ripped across the front as the bullets hit and bounced off.

He let out an enormous laugh and ripped open his shirt with his huge hands to reveal a Kevlar vest.

Rosaria's eyes clouded. It sank in. Bulletproof.

The grip on her M-16 tightened, and the soft feminine lines of her face hardened in determination.

She raised her M-16 high. High high up to the giant's face. It was a big target.

But it was too late.

Jeremiah let out another enormous laugh.

Automatic-rifle fire tore up the doorway and ripped into Rosaria's back.

Her face contorted in agony as the rifle slipped in her weakening hands. She began to crumple but forced herself to turn and face her attacker.

The black-uniformed guard stood outside the door, his eyes blank, expressionless, without emotion. He said nothing.

Only Jeremiah's laughter and the humming water pumps echoed in the room.

Rosaria went down, her rifle clattering to the floor.

RIFLE FIRE WAS COMING FROM SOMEWHERE VERY CLOSE as Barrabas scrambled down the hillside. The roof of the first building came into view. The hill was steep, dropping six feet to a long deck off the house. He jumped.

He saw the guard at the door of the building while he was in the air. More were coming up the stairs from the other house.

He started firing before he hit the ground. The guard at the door fell back inside, his hands flailing at the lead surprise.

Barrabas landed knees bent and stayed low, raising his Armalite and firing at the stairs. Four of them ran up, and the first two started firing. They caught bullets and tumbled back down the staircase. The other two turned to hightail it back down. Barrabas kept firing. The two enemy soldiers rolled the rest of the way, dead.

Then he heard a roar, something almost inhuman. He turned and saw a giant rushing him from the door of the building. The man's enormous face was bent and twisted in a horrible rage.

Finally he got to meet Jeremiah. There was no time for introductions.

Barrabas fired a 3-round burst. The 5.56mm bullets bounced off the man's chest. He saw the Kevlar vest and fired again at the head.

The long arm of Jeremiah reached out and tore the M-16 from his hands.

The giant grabbed him in a bear hug, pinning his arms to his sides. Barrabas was a big man, but Jeremiah definitely had the advantage.

Barrabas drove his fist into Jeremiah's groin, forcing the man's hips back and his body to bend forward. Then he drove his knee up into the groin. Hard.

The giant released him and howled in agony. He let go of the M-16, doubled over in pain.

Barrabas smashed the M-16 like a bat against the side of his head.

Jeremiah snapped.

He looked up at Barrabas from his doubled-over position, his eyes bulging white, his mouth foaming in rage.

"Come to me and I will crush you," he snarled.

Again Barrabas saw the livid face loom up against his as the giant reached down, his rage taking him beyond pain.

He felt the giant's vast hands encircle his neck. With his right hand Barrabas reached up to the giant's right wrist. He drove the palm of his left hand against his elbow joint, and with Jeremiah's right hand anchored to his shoulder, he put the pressure on the elbow joint.

Jeremiah was big, but he was built like everyone else.

He let go with his left hand and shrieked again in agony. Barrabas delivered a hard blow to his right elbow joint. The giant sprawled flat on the ground.

Barrabas dived for Jeremiah's back to lock him down, but the giant rolled too fast for him. He came up facing Barrabas, his back to the water pipes leading from the pumphouse to the camp below.

He was breathing heavily.

"Come on, Jeremiah." Barrabas feigned an advance and jumped back. "Come on." He motioned forward with his hands, taunting him. "Come on, get me," he challenged, moving back and forth quickly on the deck, in and out of the giant's range.

The giant lunged forward and then made a surprise move. He kicked at Barrabas's groin.

Big mistake.

Barrabas grabbed the enormous foot and twisted, throwing the giant off balance.

Jeremiah spun around backward, facing over the side of the deck, looking down at the water pipes.

Barrabas pushed the leg forward.

Jeremiah plunged headfirst over the edge.

He put out his arms to stop himself. Too late.

He crashed down off the deck and onto the water pipes leading from the pumphouse. It was a short fall, but his enormous weight crashed against the water-supply lines carrying the poisoned water down the slopes of the volcano to the suicide scene on the plaza below.

The severed pipes gushed water over the hillside and over Jeremiah. The giant lifted himself, gasping for air.

It was Barrabas's turn to kick. He kicked Jeremiah hard in the face, knocking his head back into the water gushing from the broken pipes.

Jeremiah choked on a faceful of it. He gasped for air again.

And swallowed a mouthful of water.

His eyes filled with horror as, choking and sputtering, he pushed himself up and clutched at his throat with his long thick fingers.

It was too late.

Suddenly he froze. His eyes protruded from his head like twin baseballs. He sucked in a great lungful of air with an agonizing grating sound.

But Jeremiah was a big man. The cyanide was working, but it worked slowly in his enormous body. And painfully.

He saw Barrabas and reached for the man.

Barrabas took a step back. Jeremiah stumbled forward, dazed, his eyes growing bigger and bigger, his breath jagged, raw, short and gasping. Again he lunged for the merc, and again Barrabas jumped back out of his reach.

Tottering as the cyanide slammed into his system, Jeremiah lost his balance and fell to his knees. His face was contorted with pain, and he clawed at his neck and chest, gasping for air. It didn't work.

With a long final exhalation, Jeremiah stiffened. He fell sideways and flopped flat on his back, legs and arms apart, his lips pulled back in a last scream of death. But no scream came. Jeremiah was dead.

Barrabas turned back to the door of the waterworks. Lee Hatton was bending over the body of Rosaria, with Manuelo grief-stricken by her side.

"Will she live?" Barrabas bent over Lee as the doctor filled a syringe with morphine and stuck it into the guerrilla's arm. She shook her head.

"I've stopped the bleeding and filled her full of morphine for the pain, but it's only a matter of time."

"Then let's get out of here. Bishop will be bringing the copter in any time now."

The hard-faced soldier bent over Rosaria's unconscious body and lifted it in his arms. Quickly they moved for the steps that led to the foot of the volcano.

NATE BECK COULDN'T BELIEVE IT. A winning streak. Every time he aimed his grenade and fired, he scored. All hits and not a single miss. Incredible. And he knew it was going to last.

The timing between him and Bishop at the controls of the helicopter was also incredible. Bishop whipped the craft around in spins so dizzying, sometimes Beck could taste the bottom of his stomach. Suddenly, on a hairpin, Bishop leveled it out, giving Beck a bird's-eye shot at the target.

Bishop grabbed madly at the collective, the helicopter spun around, and Beck swallowed his stomach again as he jammed another grenade onto the rifle launcher.

The scene on the ground below them was madness.

They could barely make out the chanting and drumbeats above the noise of the helicopter. But they could sure as hell see the people running like ants across the ground and dropping like dead flies. The ground was littered with bodies.

Beck stuck the barrel out the window and aimed at a half-dozen of Jeremiah's soldiers heading straight for O'Toole and Hayes, who were fighting their way in from the fence. He pulled the trigger.

The grenade smiled and waved goodbye as it soared off. Direct hit. The enemy soldiers scattered dead along the ground. O'Toole and Hayes were too busy to even look up.

Beck could see Nanos and Billy Two on the other side of the camp closing in toward the center. The sound of rifle fire became more sporadic as the SOBs wiped out the resistance and the resistance wiped itself out.

"Let's get down there and get them out," Bishop shouted at Beck above the noise of the engine.

"If we can find a place to land between all the bodies," said Beck.

Bishop was skimming over the roofs of the buildings toward the central plaza when they saw the U.S. government helicopter lift off the ground.

"Who the hell is that?" asked Bishop.

Beck peered out the windshield. He could see Nanos and Billy Two rounding the corner of a building. Nanos went down on one knee and started firing at the copter. Billy Two threw a grenade.

The copter was up. The grenade went off, but the aircraft rose into the air and headed east.

"Doesn't matter who! Our boys were shooting at it, so let's get it!" Beck was excited as hell. He slid back the door of the BK-117 to give himself a clear view.

Bishop adjusted the controls and pulled the helicopter back up again, increasing the collective for speed and putting forward pressure on the cyclic for altitude. The BK swooped up at the escaping helicopter.

Bishop dropped the nose and brought his craft parallel to the other copter as if passing a car on the highway. Beck turned sideways with his M-16 out in front and braced himself.

"Beam." Looking across, he could clearly make out the blond hair and the face he recognized from photos at the briefing session.

Beam saw his pursuer and pulled the nose of his helicopter up into a turn. Bishop swerved around. Nothing could outmaneuver a BK-117. Beam looked quickly. Beck could see panic written all over his face.

He aimed at the fuselage. And fired.

The grenade soared across the airspace between the two helicopters like a knock-out punch.

It went in the open window, across the pilot's seat and out the window on the other side.

The heat from the speeding grenade singed Beam's eyebrows.

Beck's mouth dropped open.

"What happened?" Bishop shouted, his hands diving along the controls.

"You won't believe it. Let's try again." Beck grabbed another grenade and shoved it onto the M-16. Bishop looked around to find Beam. The escaping helicopter had descended and crossed under the BK-117. He was making a run for the south.

Bishop scrambled to pull the craft around in hot pursuit.

"Shit. I don't believe it." Beck pointed out the windshield.

"What?" said Bishop. Then he saw it.

Another helicopter heading in from the south like a bat out of hell.

"Getting crowded up here," Bishop said under his breath.

The third copter was heading straight for Beam, and Beam saw it. He turned and hightailed north, crossing back toward Jeremiah's camp. The new copter closed in on his tail.

Bishop swerved the BK-117 around to avoid what looked like a certain collision. The third copter turned sideways, and an M-16 appeared at the door. A fat man braced against the seat was leaning far out of the fuselage with it. He had the M-16 up on his shoulder and aimed for Beam's helicopter. His movements were calm and deliberate, the sign of a professional.

Beam took his copter low, barely twenty feet above the ground, and was zooming back in over the New Society camp.

Orange kisses smacked from the barrel as the M-16

spat across the blue sky. The fat man with the gun was going for the rotor of the escaping craft.

He hit it.

The rotor blew off in a burst of broken metal, spun in the air and fell. The helicopter pitched out of control. Lacking torque to counterbalance the pull of the main rotor, the fuselage began to turn heavily in the opposite direction. There was no way Beam could control it.

The helicopter turned sideways, and the door opened. Beam fell out. He dropped like a stone.

But he didn't hit the ground.

He landed on the perimeter fence, caught by the spiraling coils and the silver blades of the razor wire.

The helicopter spun off until it hit the ground sideways, bounced and exploded in the river.

The other helicopter had turned and was heading down for the central plaza in the camp. The pilot, an old man with long white hair, threw them a wave and a smile before turning away.

BARRABAS LOOKED UP AT THE FENCE where the razor wire coiled wickedly. Sunlight glinted off the sharp silver blades strung along the wire.

Beam was trapped there, his body impaled on the sharp spikes at the top of the steel fence and held in place by the razors that caught at his clothing and tore his skin.

He moaned in pain, barely able to move, pinned by the deadly blades and disabled by bones broken in the fall.

Beam wasn't cool anymore. He pleaded. The words drifted across the camp, small and pathetic.

"Help me," he said.

Funny, thought Barrabas. These guys are so tough as long as they got a gun in their hand and they're sneaking up on you when your back's turned.

He felt the presence of the SOBs as they gathered around him. On the plaza behind them, the helicopters were landing.

A deathly silence had descended over Jeremiah's New Society.

It was a dead place.

Hundreds of bodies, clothed in black, lay piled on the square in great long rows, tumbled over one another as if the wind of death had swept through a field of people. The hot tropical sun beat down with a vengeance. The first vultures already swooped lazily overhead. Soon, very soon, the bodies would swell in the heat. The stench would be overwhelming.

"Help me," sobbed the man on the razor wire. He was pathetic.

Barrabas stared.

The mercs stood behind their leader and waited.

They were itching. They could pick him off bit by bit. Aim and fire. Blow off an arm, a leg. Let him bleed. Blow off something else.

Die, Beam. Die slowly for all the death you've caused. For the suffering. Your pain now is nothing to what you owe.

There wasn't a warrior among them who didn't think it. Who wasn't tempted. But they were warriors, not sadists. To defeat the evil of men like Jeremiah and Beam, it wasn't good enough to just pay in kind.

Barrabas raised his M-16. For Lopez, he thought. He shot Beam once in the head. The body jerked and fell back on the razor wire. The coil shimmered up and down the fence.

The mercs breathed again. Released.

Barrabas turned away in time to see Walker Jessup and Silver John emerge from the copter.

Silver John traveled across the plaza toward Barrabas as fast as his stiff leg could go.

"Some show you put on here, Nile." The old man approached Barrabas.

"Good to have you part of the effort again," he said. Jessup came up behind him. Barrabas reached his hand forward to shake.

"A surprise, Jessup."

"I got a little worried when I heard the senator was coming down this way," the Texan drawled. "Should've known you'd do all right without me."

Jessup looked around him. "I ain't never seen it like this," he said.

"Senator's up there." Barrabas pointed to the house on the slope of the volcano. "He's dead. They're all dead."

The Fixer nodded.

"Well, I suggest we get out of here and leave the mess for someone else to clean up. They'll think some story up for the newspapers to print. But I don't want your name in it."

"I don't want my name in it, either," said Barrabas. He shouted orders at his soldiers. "Nanos, Billy, Hayes, O'Toole—pull out with Silver John and we'll rendezvous in Panama City."

Silver John gave a big smile. "Drinks are on the house at the Starlight Lounge!"

"Sounds mighty good," said O'Toole.

"You got any women there?" Nanos asked.

"Sure do, boys. All you want," Silver John said. Jessup grimaced at his memory of what he'd seen there. Nanos was in for a big surprise.

Barrabas walked to the helicopter. Lee Hatton knelt over Rosaria, who was propped up against the wall of the fuselage. Barrabas leaned over her and met the woman warrior's fading eyes.

"We did it, Rosaria. Thanks."

She swallowed with difficulty.

"It is good." Her voice was weak. "You are a man of great courage. All of you. If only—" Her face twisted in sudden pain. "If only you were fighting on our side, Nile Barrabas. It would be better."

She smiled at him.

Barrabas brushed the hair back from the woman's forehead. He took her hand and held it.

"Rosaria, maybe we're on different sides of the fence, but I get the feeling we both believe in the same thing."

The woman's hand gripped his tightly. She closed her eyes and her body sank back, the breath leaving gently. Lee held the wrist of the other hand, probing for a pulse.

"She's gone," said Lee.

Barrabas folded the amazon's hand across her chest. He got up and moved to the copilot's seat beside Bishop, then turned to the pilot.

"Take her up," he said. "The war is over."

TIMES SQUARE. DUSK. The lights coming on. Barrabas stood there again and watched. Back in America, a long way from that Honduran hell. One more thing to do and then he could forget about it.

He walked to a phone booth on the corner of Forty-second Street and asked the operator for Amsterdam.

He could hear it ringing in the eighteenth-century town house in the Begijne Hof. A silky voice answered sleepily.

"I'm in New York."

He heard her sharp intake of breath. Something he knew she'd never say. That she'd been waiting to know if he were dead or alive.

"Well, come on over." Erika's soft laughter danced in his ear.

"Soon," he said. He hung up and pulled the paper

from his pocket. The address was on the Lower East Side. Way downtown. Not a nice part of New York. The part where poor people lived. People like Emilio Lopez's family.

They weren't poor anymore. Lopez had left them a bundle. He'd go down and tell the dead man's mother that she was rich now.

Big deal. She'd lost her son.

It was a long way from the Times Square phone booth to the tenement on the Lower East Side. Miles.

Barrabas walked.

JACK HILD

Though still an American citizen, Jack Hild no longer resides in the United States. His current whereabouts are unknown. No one associated with Gold Eagle Books has ever seen Jack, in person or in a photograph, or has ever spoken to him directly. His publishers deal with him through a European attorney-agent who forwards contracts, checks, fan mail. If you should ever meet Jack Hild—and are sure that it's really him—let us know. We'd like to hear about it!

SOBs

#5 GULAG WAR

by Jack Hild

MORE GREAT ACTION COMING SOON!

Nobody breaks *into* Siberia . . . except Nile Barrabas and his SOBs!

Their mission is to flatten one of the Soviet Union's most inhuman concentration camps, in order to free a very special prisoner. But the SOBs' incursion into the USSR is discovered early in the game. The Russians know the Americans are inside and play a waiting game to find out their target.

Somebody should have told Barrabas that *nobody* breaks into Siberia! Nobody, that is, in his right mind. . . .

Available soon wherever paperbacks are sold.

HE'S EXPLOSIVE. HE'S MACK BOLAN... AGAINST ALL ODDS

He learned his deadly skills in Vietnam...then put them to good use by destroying the Mafia in a blazing one-man war. Now **Mack Bolan** ventures further into the cold to take on his deadliest challenge yet—the KGB's worldwide terror machine.

Follow the lone warrior on his exciting new missions...and get ready for more nonstop action from his high-powered combat teams: **Able Team**—Bolan's famous Death Squad—battling urban savagery too brutal and volatile for regular law enforcement. And **Phoenix Force**—five extraordinary warriors handpicked by Bolan to fight the dirtiest of antiterrorist wars, blazing into even greater danger.

Fight alongside these three courageous forces for freedom in all-new action-packed novels! Travel to the gloomy depths of the cold Atlantic, the scorching sands of the Sahara, and the desolate Russian plains. You'll feel the pressure and excitement building page after page, with nonstop action that keeps you enthralled until the explosive conclusion!

Now you can have all the new Gold Eagle novels delivered right to your home!

You won't want to miss a single one of these exciting new action-adventures. And you don't have to! Just fill out and mail the card at right, and we'll enter your name in the Gold Eagle home subscription plan. You'll then receive six brand-new action-packed Gold Eagle books every other month, delivered right to your home! You'll get two Mack Bolan novels, one Able Team and one Phoenix Force, plus one book each from two thrilling, new Gold Eagle libraries, **SOBs** and **Track**. In **SOBs** you'll meet the legendary team of mercenary warriors who fight for justice and win. **Track** features a military and weapons genius on a mission to stop a maniac whose dream is everybody's worst nightmare. Only Track stands between us and nuclear hell!

FREE! The New War Book and Mack Bolan bumper sticker.

As soon as we receive your card we'll rush you the long-awaited New War Book and Mack Bolan bumper sticker—both ABSOLUTELY FREE. Then under separate cover, you'll receive your six Gold Eagle novels.

The New War Book is *packed* with exciting information for Bolan fans: a revealing look at the hero's life...two new short stories...book character biographies...even a combat catalog describing weapons used in the novels! The New War Book is a special collector's item you'll want to read again and again. And it's yours FREE when you mail your card!

Of course, you're under no obligation to buy anything. Your first six books come on a 10-day free trial—if you're not thrilled with them, just return them and owe nothing. The New War Book and bumper sticker are yours to keep, FREE!

Don't miss a single one of these thrilling novels...mail the card now, while you're thinking about it.

HE'S UNSTOPPABLE.
AND HE'LL FIGHT
TO DEFEND FREEDOM!

Mail this coupon today!